SUCKER FOR PAIN

REBEL PR BOOK 1

SUSAN HARRIS

SUCKER FOR PAIN
Copyright ©2024 Susan Harris

Originally published as Kindle Vella Episodes

Cover Design by: Gem Promotions
Typography by: Gem Promotions

Prologue

Shane

"And now, on the rings, representing the Republic of Ireland, Shane Carter."

Shane's heart was racing.

This was it. This was the culmination of the years of training, the early mornings, the torn muscles, the loneliness, and the constant scrutiny from his dad.

Shane stepped onto the mat, ignoring the pang of hunger in his stomach and the twinge in his shoulder. He lifted his hand up as he faced the judges and then readied himself to be hoisted up by his trainer. Firm hands gripped his waist as he heard his dad mutter. "Don't fuck this up, lad."

Shane flinched. There was never any congratulations or praise when your dad was your trainer. Just you didn't hit that quite right. You should have stuck the landing better. You're late for training when you arrive at five o one instead of five.

Shane tried to drown out his dad as he grabbed the rings. The moment his fingers grasped them, the world almost fell away. In the quiet and the familiarity of the routine, Shane almost felt like he had control over his life.

When he was up here, there was no watching of calories, no dad lecturing him about his eating, or his exercise regime. There was no hiding his injuries, no hiding the junk food stashed under his bed that he binged on minutes before he vomited it all back up again. No hiding the fact that the sport he used to love had become something that he loathed.

Almost as much as he hated his dad.

He needed to concentrate now. Ignore the pain in his shoulder. Ignore the way his heart was racing and the dizziness that made the arena spin. This was the Olympics. Failure was not an option.

Weakness was never an option.

Shane went through his routine like he had a million times before. The bite of pain helped him focus as he transitioned into more difficult moves. The pain intensified in his shoulder as he moved from a Butterfly to V-Cross, then into a handstand. His arms shook with the strain. He tried to focus his eyes on the crowd to get some motivation.

He continued the routine, went into his swings and then went into a planchet. His shoulder screamed as he swung again trying to hit another handstand before he went into an Iron Cross. The nausea, the dizziness, and the searing pain intensified and Shane tried to block it out. He came out of the Iron Cross, swinging into another handstand.

Something tore in his shoulder, and he bit his tongue to stop from crying out. The world around Shane swayed as his body gave out. He plummeted to the mat, hitting so hard that the sound echoed even as his body rippled with pain. He tried to get up, but it was like his body wouldn't listen to him as Shane heard the shocked gasps and the calls as he tried to push off the mat and failed.

They'll all know now...they'll know you're weak...

His dad's voice in his head was the last thing Shane heard before he blacked out.

CHAPTER ONE

Shane

EIGHT YEARS Later

Andrea fucking Collins was the devil dressed in a power suit and heels.

For years now, the harpy who was one of his closest friends, had been trying to get him to move home to Ireland and take over some clientele out of the Cork branch of Rebel PR. Shane had venomously refused to do that, but Andi had made it her life's mission to get him to come around.

It wasn't Andi's fault that she didn't know all the reasons why Shane had never wanted to step foot in Cork again.

But here he was, on a plane back to the place he'd grown up, to have it out with Andi about her tactics. When Andi and Charlie had returned to Cork and decided that Rebel PR's head office should be there, and the Manchester office scaled down, Shane had been happy to stay in Manchester and oversee things, especially when Charlie took a step back from Rebel PR to run Rebel Racers, the Formula 1 team that she'd inherited.

Both Andi and Charlie had come home and found love, and then Andi had decided to hound him. Shane had done everything he could to persuade her that he didn't want to come back to the place that held so many demons that it made Shane feel on edge.

But Andi had taken away his clients. And she'd not given him any new ones. Andi had basically demoted him to receptionist and chef tea and coffee maker. Shane had dug his heels in for weeks and pretended that the hours of mindless boredom weren't driving him slowly insane.

Shane had tried to keep to his routine. Wake up, work out, eat breakfast, go to work, have lunch, work more, home, dinner, light stretching and either binge a show or do something with Ronan.

Ronan Cusack was his best friend, had been since they were both in secondary school together. Ronan had been catapulted into stardom starring in a TV series just as Shane was starting to make waves in the gymnastics world. They understood each other and being thrown into the spotlight.

Now even Ronan had ended up falling for a feisty woman who Shane would never have put the shy, almost reserved actor with. Shane liked Sorcha, but it also meant that now his best mate had decided as well that Cork was where he needed to be.

Ronan was one of the few people who knew what had really happened In Brazil at the Olympics and the aftermath. Neither Andi or Charlie, or any of their college classmates knew. If there was anything good that Henry Carter had done in his life, it was to cover up just how ill his son had been, redirecting blame on his physio's mistreatment of a shoulder injury. That was the public story of how his career had ended. And one of the reasons he had not seen his dad in almost eight years.

Shane often wondered what his life would have been like if his mam had stuck around and not gotten sick of the way his dad had treated them both. She'd been depressed and left when Shane was eleven, though as much as Shane would have wished that she had taken him with her, he knew his dad would never have allowed it.

It was one of the things that he and Charlie had shared. Mothers who left them with their fathers and made new families for themselves. But while Philip Coyle had been a loving father, Henry Carter had emotionally and mentally abused him into becoming the perfect athlete.

No matter what it cost.

No matter what it cost *Shane*.

No matter that it had almost cost him his life.

It had sent him on a one-way ticket out of Cork, with no plans to ever return. He'd made quick trips to Dublin or Belfast for sporting events his clients had been taking part in. But he'd avoided Cork like the plague and had created a life for himself that didn't involve gymnastics, or the horrible aftermath.

You let me down, lad. This was your shot.

I can't believe that you were so weak. Disgracing me on national TV.

Little sissy boy who couldn't even push through a little pain.

Shane wished he was anywhere but on this fucking plane bound for Cork.

Scrubbing a hand down his face, Shane turned his head and looked out the window. He'd been fuming since the plane ticket had arrived on his desk, complete with a note saying that it was time that he was done dossing, stop avoiding her, and get his ass on the flight.

Shane had wanted to dig his heels in and refuse. But he needed to be kept occupied. If left to get lost in his thoughts, Shane dwelled on things. He obsessed about things in his past and that never did any good. Then Charlie had called him and asked him to come back since she wasn't allowed to fly in the last few months of her pregnancy, and Noah would be leaving soon for preseason testing.

"If you just let Andi give her full pitch and still say no, she'll ease up. Right now, she just feels like you are saying no because it's her asking you."

Shane had snorted. "She's not asking, Charlie, she's forcing my hand. Bulldozing through to get her own way like she always does."

Charlie had laughed, rolling her eyes. "That's Andi. But that same take-no-prisoners attitude just means she cares. Besides, Shane, you are the best PR sportsperson we have at Rebel PR and Andi wants the best working for her in Cork. She knows she's terrible with sports and that I'm only interested in motorsport, so she needs you for everything else."

Charlie had gone on to tell Shane that Andi wanted him to be head of their sports division. He would have people working for him, and his personal pick of clients. That the first person on his books would be Emil Anderson, Danish Football captain and premier league player. And that Luke Sullivan and Jack O'Neill would need looking after when they started their rally careers. Charlie was baiting him with high-profile clients so that Andi could reel him in with her pitch.

While Andi was blunt and forward, Charlie was subtle and charming. Andi was the type of forward who walked up to rockstars and movie stars as a newbie PR CEO and managed to walk out with signed contracts. Charlie was the one who smiled and laughed, and then told someone all the reasons why signing with them was the best thing for their career. There was a reason why they were Internationally recognised as the best PR company, and two of them had been named in numerous most powerful women in business lists.

He'd known that they would do great things when they presented a group project about a PR company and that was the foundation for Rebel PR. Not only that, but Andi had been the first person to invite him on one of their nights out, not taking no for an answer. They'd gone to the bar that Andi worked in, and they'd treated Shane like he'd been one of them all along.

Andi and Charlie had no idea who he was at the time. He'd been embarrassed when someone had figured out who he was, or rather who he'd once been. An Olympian who had suffered a career-ending injury that happened to have been shown on international TV.

After that, they'd still not treated him any differently but worked him into their plans for world domination. He'd been happy, and content with his new career until Andi started to talk about bringing Rebel PR back where it was always supposed to be.

Having people around him that didn't want anything from him other than his friendship, was a strange yet joyful thing for Shane. Apart from Ronan, people had always wanted something from him. His dad wanted that gold medal to brag to all his friends about. His sponsors wanted him to look good in their clothes, shoes, and magazine covers.

There had been many a time that Shane had felt guilty for not telling Andi and even Charlie the truth, and many a time he had come close to confiding in them the reason why sometimes he turned down invites to dinners, why he sometimes didn't answer any messages for days.

But admitting it out loud might give it more power. Besides, he'd hate for people to start looking at him differently. He'd worked too hard to have the life he had now. He liked living in Manchester, his work, and his friends.

CHAPTER TWO

Shane

SHANE HADN'T KNOWN the effect that his dad would have on him over the years. Growing up, he'd thought all parents were like his dad. He assumed that getting up at five am to train, his dad counting his calorie intake, the twice daily weigh-ins that sometimes led to an extra training session if Henry Carter thought Shane was even a pound over the optimal target weight, was normal

His obsession with food started back then. Well, that's what his psychologist at the treatment facility had said. His dad used to send him to bed hungry sometimes if he was overweight or hadn't had the perfect routine locked down. Shane learned to hide food away, and he'd started bingeing on the stolen treats when his dad starved him.

Shane had also started to weigh himself before his morning and evening check-ins with his dad. If he was overweight, Shane would make himself sick in the hopes it would work and when it did, the relief was so intense that Shane started to repeat the process.

He'd researched online ways to lose weight fast. Once, after he and Ronan had gone to a movie and eaten greasy food, Shane had felt so disgusted with himself that he'd stopped at the chemist on the way home and taken a handful of the laxatives.

His dad had been away for work, so it had been easy to hide what he had done.

Shane had become an expert at hiding his behaviours, so much so that his dad had never noticed his constant sore throats from vomiting, the tablets he took for acid reflux, or anything like that. Even when he'd had what felt like a heart attack, the doctor had put it down to the rush of adrenaline and dismissed any other issues.

No one saw what was happening to him, or more like they didn't want to fucking see it.

Even the injury to his shoulder was ignored when the Olympics neared. He'd been given injections to keep him going. The pain coupled with the continuous pressure from his dad had led him to days of starving himself, then eating so much that it was no hardship to vomit it all back up.

So, Shane had gone to the Olympics. He'd already secured medals on individual apparatus but had missed out on gold, so the last all rounds were his chance to get that medal his dad wanted. He'd already secured enough marks to medal but needed a good score to stand on top of the podium.

He'd almost done it. He'd almost made it through the routine and would have done so if his shoulder hadn't given out. He'd blacked out when he'd hit the mat and when he'd woken in the hospital alone, he'd had to ask a nurse when she came in if he had gotten gold.

The nurse had seen the anguish in his eyes and touched his arm. It had been so long since someone had touched him with kindness that he'd broken down in tears. The nurse had sat with him, holding his hand until his dad had come in, took one look at Shane, and then walked right back out.

His dad didn't speak to him for the two days he was in hospital while they ran tests. Then just before he was discharged, the doctor called him and his dad into a room and Shane's world crashed down around him.

"We believe your son has bulimia nervosa."

Shane swallowed hard. Now all the questions made sense. They were digging around to find out what fucking mental disorder he had. They'd been struggling to understand how someone as fit and seemingly healthy as Shane had damaged his shoulder so badly.

Apparently, the instability in his shoulder could be a factor that was exasperated by his bulimia.

His dad snorted. "Only fucking girls have bulimia."

The doctor looked at Shane before sliding his unimpressed gaze to his dad. "That is simply not true. Men and boys are less likely to be diagnosed because of the stigma and such thinking. Shane's illness has been assessed and he has bulimia,"

"He's an athlete, doctor. Not some headcase."

The doctor looked at Shane and Shane lowered his gaze so the doctor would not see the truth. God, his dad was gonna be insufferable now. He'd watch Shane like a hawk. He'd force him to eat and train and he would never have a moment's peace from it all.

"Your son is not a headcase as you put it, Mr. Carter. He had developed an illness due to the pressures of being an athlete. His illness is manageable with the right course of treatment."

His dad shook his head. "Don't talk about shit that isn't true. Tell me how long before his shoulder is healed enough to restart his training. Tell me what he has to do to defend his European title. Tell me how to make sure that he doesn't fuck up again and becomes a proper Olympian."

"Mr. Carter, I assure you that your son is a proper

Olympian. And perhaps it would be best if you focus on getting your son well before you put him back into the very atmosphere that had led us to the here and now."

Shane lifted his eyes at the sharpness in the woman's tone and he gave her a weak smile. Fuck, when was the last time someone had his back other than Ronan? When was the last time he felt valued for more than medals and accolades?

His dad got up so fast off his chair that it scraped, and Shane winced. "You don't get to tell me how to raise my son. Let's go, lad."

His dad had stormed from the room, leaving Shane to slowly rise.

"Shane."

He looked at the doctor who smiled and handed him a card. "If you want to talk, you can call me. I'm going back to Ireland after the games close out so call me. I'm here for you."

Shane never had, but after confiding in Ronan, his friend had forced him to get some help. He'd let Shane crash at his place, but wouldn't let Shane hide his eating disorder. Ronan's parents had taken him to see a doctor friend of theirs and Shane admitted that he'd been diagnosed with bulimia.

He'd been admitted to a treatment facility the next day by the doctor and not even his dad could fight against it. He couldn't leave. It was a compulsory order as the doctor felt that both Shane's mental and physical health were in danger of being affected even more so under the care of his father.

It had been the best thing for him. Shane had learned to accept he had an eating disorder and techniques to manage it. He ate meals in public for the first time in what felt like forever. The doctors at the facility gave him a routine that he still followed to this day, including rest days from exercise.

Shane wouldn't say that he was cured, no, he'd always be bulimic, but he knew how to manage it now, and he knew when things started to slide, and he needed help.

The guidance counselor in the facility told him that he could be a gymnast again, if that was what he wanted, or he could do something else. All Shane knew was sport. And he wanted out of Ireland. He was too well known in Cork, and he couldn't heal here. He picked Manchester on a whim because he followed Manchester United growing up and the PR course looked like something he could do while he was deciding on his future.

Shane would never have believed that seven years after he left, he'd end back up where he started. A knot lodged in his stomach as the plane landed and he grabbed his gear bag and exited the plane. He pulled his baseball cap down low over his forehead as he passed the photos of great athletes and flinched at the picture of himself.

It felt like yesterday and a lifetime ago all rolled into one.

Shane strode out of the arrivals and jerked his head up when he heard a shrill whistle. Andrea "Andi" Collins stood off to the side with the smuggest grin on her face at his arrival. Of course, she'd be waiting for him here. Andi would want to make sure that he didn't turn right around and get on a plane before she'd had her chance to pitch to him.

"Carter." She said her gin deepening.

"Collins." Shane replied with a sort of growl as he shifted the weight of his gear bag.

Andi pointed to the bag. "That all you got?"

"I'm not staying long." Shane told her and that only made her grin even more.

"Sure, you are. But let's get ya out of the airport so you can't run away. I've got shit to show ya, Carter. And you're gonna love it!"

He doubted that. He doubted that very fucking much.

Chapter Three

Eve

Her feet slapped against the pavement as she ran, her lungs burning, and her muscles screaming at her. But Eve was used to pushing her body to the limit, and then pushing some more. She needed to keep her stamina up because she needed to bring her A game in the Octagon. If you didn't go to war ready to win, then you would end up on your ass and Eve Andrews did not let anyone put her on the mat like that.

Having spent the last few years training in Next Gen MMA with some of the best fighters in the UK, Eve had come home after signing with Rebel PR. She'd been homesick for a while, even though the plane journey to visit was a quick one. However, after her gran had died, even though she wasn't her gran by blood, and all the shit happened with her cousin Darren, Eve had been eager to come back to Ireland.

Signing her contract in Liverpool to have Rebel PR represent her and try and get her on some big cards had been an exciting time for her, especially when Andi Collins had told her that Noah Donovan and Andi's fiancé, rockstar Declan

Walsh had opened an elite gym in Cork and that she had unlimited access as part of her contract.

Andi had also set her up with a sweet apartment right across from the gym. When Noah and Declan had started to buy up all the buildings in the industrial estate, they had converted lots of space into apartments so that athletes and recording artists had places to stay considering Declan's studio was right next door to the gym and the Rebel PR offices.

Declan and Andi lived across the way from her, and Andi's brother and Declan's bandmate Rhys lived above the gym with his girlfriend Shay Gleeson, who worked with her cousin Darren. It all seemed like it was too perfect but hey, if it meant she didn't have to move back in with her mam and dad, that was a bonus. She loved her parents, but she had lived by herself for so long that there was no way she could go back to the fussing and her mam's reaction to her black eyes and bruises.

Eve sighed as she pushed open the door to her apartment and went to the fridge to get a bottle of water. She guzzled half of it as she checked her phone and saw a text from her mam asking her if she wanted to go shopping with her and go for afternoon tea.

Feeling just a twinge of guilt, Eve texted her mam back and said she had a meeting this afternoon with Andi to discuss some appearances. It was half the truth. Andi had told her to hang around the gym because she was going to be showing around the person who was going to be managing her account.

Eve had protested a little and asked why Andi couldn't manage her, but Andi told her that she was clueless when it came to anything sports and this person had managed premier league footballers, both men and women, and lots of other sportspeople.

That eased her trepidation a little. At least the person

would be professional. Perhaps this person wouldn't look at her and see the blond hair and small frame and wonder why the fuck was Barbie trying to make it in MMA.

Darren always told her that she was five foot three with a six-foot attitude. That was the perfect way to describe her. The trainers in Liverpool told her she was like a Jack Russell, yappy and never fucking let go once she sank her teeth in. Eve used her looks to fool people into underestimating her. She'd taken down bigger and bulkier opponents because they just saw a pretty face before she knocked them clean out.

Her mam had been appalled when she had asked to learn how to box, opting to send Eve to ballet instead. She hated it, and even at seven, knew that she'd never be a prima ballerina. She'd kept up the lessons after bribing her mam and dad to let her go to a boxing gym.

A year later she won her first medal and the thrill of it had her hooked.

Eve devoured everything fight-related. She studied all kinds of martial arts, watching online videos and practicing at home. She'd taken self-defence classes and asked to be taught moves she'd seen women online do. When she managed to take down a boy in one of her classes and twisted his arm making him tap, one of the teachers who taught MMA approached her and asked if he could train her.

It had taken a lot of convincing, especially since it was suggested was the best place for Eve to learn was in Liverpool. Her parents had wanted her to finish school, so she had a tutor in Liverpool so she could train. There would be no college for her once school was done because Eve wanted to main stage a fight. She needed to learn all she could, and she'd never been academic anyways.

Eve had had a few fights, and was undefeated, but she was struggling to book anything that would get her in front of the right people. Sponsorships were hard to come by and that's why she'd decided to put faith in Rebel PR. She was twenty-three years old. She was fit and healthy but even she knew she only had a few good years of MMA before she'd have to rethink her options.

Fighting was all she knew.

She changed out of her running gear and into her workout gear before heading over to the gym. She scanned her card and went in, thrilled to see that it was empty save for Noah who waved at her from the office. Eve had only been working out here a few weeks but everyone knew her routine. She almost laughed as Noah got up and closed the office door. Eve stripped off her jumper and tossed that and her bag to the side.

She stretched out her limbs, making sure she was ready before she hooked her phone up to the stereo system and cranked up the hip-hop tunes. She saw Noah shaking his head in the office and Eve laughed. They'd had a long conversation about music when she'd first rocked up and saw him working out to techno music. She'd asked him why he was here instead of the state-of-the-art gym at the Rebel Racers facility, and he'd admitted that he was supposed to be having the week off and he'd come here pretending he needed to do paperwork.

Eve had laughed, understanding completely. She got angsty herself if she wasn't working out and when she told Noah that she got restless when she wasn't fighting, he offered to spar with her. She'd been skeptical until the very next day she'd come to work out and seen Noah and Quinn Murphy sparring. Hell, she'd even sparred with Quinn.

That woman hit hard, and Eve was happy to reciprocate.

Even the watchful glare of Quinn's race manager and boyfriend Oskar hadn't deterred them. So she sparred once or twice a week with the Rebel Racer's crew. Quinn wanted Eve to teach her a few MMA moves and even Noah had watched intently, just rolling his eyes when Eve winked at Quinn and told her that some of the moves worked great in bed too.

Quinn had gone red as Oskar just rolled his eyes. It was nice to hang out with people who were athletes like her, but in another aspect of it so there was no competition. Sometimes in Liverpool, it felt like the girls were intimidated by her and the boys just wanted to fuck her. That had been part of the reason she'd wanted to come home.

Even with her mam's nagging, and constant need to try and get Eve to be more girlie, it was worth it. She got to hang with her fave cousin, and train with really famous sports people. She had made more friends in the last couple of weeks than in all her years in Liverpool. This felt like the right fit for her.

Now, if only she could get on someone's radar and get offered a big fight.

This was her time to shine. She had to take this shot and run with it. She would prepare herself mentally and physically, and when the time came, she would walk into the octagon and fight for her right to be up there with the best.

Eve turned up the volume of M.I.A's *Bad Girls* and got to work, grinning as Noah pulled on his headphones in the office. Then she blocked out everything else and sat down on the first apparatus. She had this ...failure was not an option.

CHAPTER FOUR

Shane

SHANE LET Andi rabbit on the entire car journey, because it was easier to just let her get it all out so that when Shane eventually turned around and told her thanks but no thanks and he was happy in Manchester, Andi couldn't turn accuse him of not even given her a chance.

He looked out the window, thinking that it looked the same and different all at once. That didn't even make sense but that was what it felt like. His knee bounced with all the pent-up anxiety and his stomach churned.

This had been a horrible idea. He should never have agreed to come.

Now, Andi was strolling around the brand new offices, that, to be fair, were bigger and nicer than the office in Manchester, and she doing her best sales pitch. So far she'd shown him the kitchen, the lounge area, the conference room, her office, Charlie's office, and then she stopped outside one of the other offices.

"And this is your office," Andi informed him with a grin.

Shane rolled his eyes. "I don't need an office, Collins."

Andi gestured around her. "I mean, the space is pretty sweet and way more room to maneuver than the old office. But me and Charlie decided that when you come home, you deserved your own office."

"If, Andi, *if*."

"Semantics." Andi replied with a snort and a grin. She started to tell him about all the new clients and the plans they had for expansion and how big of a factor Shane was in their plans.

Shane leaned against one of the desks and braced his hands on the edge. Andi propped herself up on one of the other desks, her steely gaze on him as she frowned.

"Come on, Carter! Give me a hint. Give me a little sliver of an expression that tells me what way you are leaning. I hate that resting bitch face of yours."

Shane sighed, crossing his legs as he folded his arms across his chest. "And I hate being manipulated into coming here because you decided that you wanted me here. Guess you can't win um all."

Andi flipped him off as the door opened and Charlie strode in. He hadn't seen her in what felt like forever. He'd spoken to her numerous times, but since announcing her pregnancy to the world in a very public way late last year, Charlie hadn't been over to Manchester too much. Charlie grinned when she saw him and Shane pushed off the desk, ready to hug her when he stopped short and looked right at the very pronounced bump.

Charlie rolled her eyes and almost growled at him. "For fuck sake, Shane, I'm not gonna break. I'm five months pregnant, not made of glass."

Shane heard the frustration in her tone, and he wondered if her fiancé was doing his overprotective thing considering he should be jetting off to start the new F1 season any day now.

Charlie was frowning and Shane hated to see her looking so off. He'd not seen her this out of sorts since Noah came back on the scene.

He tilted his head and gave her a lopsided grin. "Nah, I was just trying to figure out if I'd manage to get me arms around you. I mean, that bump's pretty much a deterrent, isn't it?"

Charlie gave him a dark look. "Oh fuck off you asshole and just hug me. Don't you know it's rude to comment on a girl's weight, even if she is pregnant?"

Shane snorted. "But you aren't a girl, Charlie. Doesn't count."

Charlie smacked him on the arm and wrapped her arms around him. Shane hugged her back, careful not to do it too tightly. Shane didn't know Noah Donovan too well, but if Charlie loved him, he must be a great guy.

Stepping out of his embrace, Charlie gripped his arms. "You look good, Shane. It's so damn good to see you."

"You'll get to see him all the time now that he's staying, Charlie."

Charlie looked over at her best friend. "I told you to go easy on him."

"And I told you that going easy hadn't gotten us anywhere the last bloody year." Andi said back to Charlie.

"Andi..." Charlie said with a sigh as she put her hand on her stomach.

"Charlie..."

Shane shook his head even as he rubbed his temple. This was like all the times in college whenever there was a disagreement, Charlie was the voice of reason, whereas Andi just talked until you saw her way of thinking. It was like no time had lapsed. The two women were glaring at each other and turned that glare on him when he cleared his throat.

"Listen, fun as this is and all," He started, shoving his

hands into his pocket, "But I heard the sales pitch and the offer of my own office. So thanks but no thanks. Now, can you stop messing with all my clients and just give me some work to do back in Manchester?"

Charlie glared at Andi. "You didn't tell him?"

Andi dismissed her with a wave of her hand. "I was getting there. But thought like show him all the new shit before I tell him the news."

Shane's stomach was already in knots but it plummeted to his feet at Andi's words.

"What news?"

Andi had the good graces to look sheepish and it took a lot to make Andi look guilty about anything. "We both, me and Charlie, made the decision to wind things down in Manchester."

Shane blinked. "Wind down? As in...?"

Charlie reached over and touched his arm. "As in close down the office in Manchester. We don't own the building like we do this place and we can always hire a meeting room if we need to. Everyone else is happy to work remotely and travel for any meetings, but we are going to have our base here, in Cork."

Shit...shit. Shit. Shit.

"So I either come work here for you guys or I'm fired, right?" Shane snapped, anger coursing through him. He felt manipulated, toyed with, and he had spent too long being manipulated by fucking people who wanted him to do things they wanted him to do.

"Shane, we are not firing you," Charlie said, resting her hands on her bump. "We would very much like you to come here and work. I need someone to take over some of my clients when I go on maternity leave, and we have been inundated with sports personalities wanting Rebel PR to represent them. Andi has already been working all hours because

I've got terrible morning sickness and she hasn't slept in weeks."

Shane glanced over at Andi, who just shrugged. "I'm fine. Charlie wouldn't have known anything but Declan bitched to Noah that I was working all hours. He shouldn't have said anything. I can handle the extra work."

Shane knew Andi was stubborn as hell and she wouldn't ask for help even if she was at death's door. He remembered one of their projects for college and Andi had a bad flu and she worked until she fell down and was carted off in an ambulance severely dehydrated.

"Look," Andi started, holding her hands up and it was the most in the way of an apology that he would ever get from the woman who *hated* to admit that she was in the wrong. "Did I go about this the wrong way? Maybe. Okay, probably. We're here, Carter. Ronan's here. I have a gaff for you to stay in so just hear me out and come and see this MMA fighter that I think you will love. They have what it takes to be the best, with the right person supporting them."

It was the look in Andi's eyes that had him nodding and following the two women next door to the gym. Andi and Charlie were chatting away about the gym, the new clients, and Shane just nodded as they led him into the gym, the music blaring from inside.

Shane looked around the gym, already a little in love with the place and then his eyes landed on the most gorgeous woman he'd ever seen in his life. She was shorter than him with abs and muscles that spoke of hours of training and he should know. Long blonde hair that was pulled back off her face and showed off her fine cheekbones, glacier-blue eyes, and full lips. She was curvy too, and right now, was bench pressing more than should be possible for her size.

Was she the MMA fighter's girlfriend?

Andi had a glint in her eyes at whatever she had seen in his expression, and he looked away from the woman as Andi said. "That's Eve Andrews, future MMA star, and hopefully your client. I told her when she signed that I would get her the best and I hate to admit it, Carter, but you are the fucking best. Just meet her before you decide on anything. *Please*."

Chapter Five

Eve

Eve had been so lost in her workout routine that it took her a while to feel the weight of eyes on her. She just assumed it was Noah or some other person who worked out at the gym and got the shock of their lives when they saw her deadlifting weights. Eve ignored whoever it was for a few more heartbeats before she finally lifted her gaze.

Standing on the other side of the gym was a man wearing the grimmest expression on his face. And damn, if it wasn't a striking face. High cheekbones cut his face in a sharp angle that should have made him look gaunt but instead it just made him more appealing. A firm jaw that was emphasised by full lips that had a faint line of stubble that was lighter than his hair. His hair was dark brown in colour to match intense eyes that were still looking at her.

Eve was around muscular men all the damn time, ones who flexed and posed when a pretty woman was around. But this man looked caged in his clothes, like it was a travesty to be wearing that snug pair of jeans and slim-fitting hoodie. She could tell that he was stacked underneath those clothes. He was all broad shoulders, slim hips, and thick thighs that would make a rugby player jealous.

He looked like he'd stepped out of an Abercrombie and Fitch catalogue.

Eve wouldn't mind peeling off those clothes and getting a better look at what was underneath.

She set down the weights and reached for the remote to turn off the music, dragging her gaze from whoever Mr. Abercrombie was. It was only then did she spot Andi, and Noah's fiancée Charlie standing beside the man. Once she turned off the music, Eve grabbed her bottle of water and took a slug before she strode over to where the others were standing.

Charlie said hi to Eve, then put her hand on the man's arm. "I'm just gonna go talk to Noah for a second. Please hear Andi out and we can talk then. Don't argue with her for the sake of it, Shane. Please."

The man, Shane, snorted, rolling his eyes but he had yet to say anything.

Charlie lifted her brows at Andi. "Don't push him, Andi. You two are as stubborn as one another and you will both dig your heels in to spite the other."

Andi pressed her lips together and Charlie just sighed before she walked off. An awkward silence fell down around them, and Eve shifted her weight on her feet, and wiped the sweat from her brow with the back of her hand. Andi and Shane looked at each other, their eyes latched in a silent battle of wills and while Eve was used to sizing up opponents and studying fighters to try and determine an outcome to a fight, she honestly couldn't tell who would win this round.

Shane lifted his arm to look at his watch and then gave Andi a bored expression that had the woman frowning and folding her arms across her chest. There was a flicker of something on Shane's lips, like he was trying not to smirk or laugh, but neither of them would give the other an inch.

"Oh for fuck sake lads, this could go on all day and I've got shit to do." Eve blurted out, rolling her eyes. Turning to the man, she held out her hand, to which he looked down at it, then back at her with that intensity still in his eyes. "Eve Andrews. Nice to meet ya."

A firm warm hand grasped hers. "Shane Carter."

His voice was deep, distinctively Corkonian, and gave Eve that kind of feeling you got when you drank hot chocolate before it had cooled. There was a flash of something in his eyes that seemed to relax after a few seconds and he removed his hand from hers.

Andi stepped forward and nudged Shane with her shoulder. "Shane went to Uni with me and Charlie. Of course, out of all the Universities in the UK, the three Cork people ended up in the same classes. We've been friends ever since."

"Not like I had a choice. You basically bullied me into doing a team project with you two."

"You were sat there like a puppy, afraid to ask anyone to join the group project," Andi said with a laugh. "I was being charitable."

"And then you tried to fix me and Charlie up." Shane retorted, and Eve watched the interaction with amusement.

"Shhh...don't let Donovan hear that. He's already all up in a heap because he has to leave in a couple weeks."

Eve glanced over her shoulder, itching to get back to work.

"Right so moving on from my really bad matchmaking skills. Shane, Eve here is the MMA fighter that I was telling you about."

Shane faced her again, this time his expression had shifted from grim to assessing. She felt like he was scrutinizing her, and she instantly tensed when it felt like this Shane was assuming the worst about her.

Hands on her hips, Eve tilted her head and cocked an eyebrow, daring him to say something. She had no problem putting him on the floor if this Shane turned out to be an asshole and looked down his nose at her.

"Eve decided to come home having been training at Next Gen MMA for the last couple of years. She's had some decent fights the past couple of years, however we can do better. I have a list of sponsorship deals that are trying to outbid one another to have Eve wearing their clothes, sneakers, and drinking their beverages."

While that was exciting and great and all, Eve was more concerned about her next fight. If she wanted to make it onto the radar of the head honchos at UFC, she needed more than a sponsorship deal with some brand that wanted her to wear their knickers.

"Eve lives in the apartment across the ways from yours," Andi said, and Eve heard the tentative tone that she was using.

"My apartment?" Shane asked deadpan, a muscle ticking in his jaw.

Andi ignored his question and continued to talk. "Shane was almost top of our class in Manchester. Behind me that is. But he is our go-to guy when it comes to anything sports-related. He works his ass off for his clients. Like legit, you couldn't have a better person repping you for Rebel PR."

Shane gave Andi a look. "You know flattery doesn't work on me, Collins."

"It's not flattery if it's the truth."

Annnnd now they were back to staring at each other, making Eve feel uncomfortable. Shane glanced at his watch again, like he had a plane to catch or something, and the look of boredom on his face was really starting to annoy the fuck out of her.

"Shane is the perfect person to help you out, Eve. And he can double as a sparring partner now that Noah and Quinn are both off to start the new season. Declan and the band are doing a few gigs in the EU so he won't be around either."

"Andi." Shane started, but that didn't stop Andi from going on.

"Like think of this as your own little training village. You have the swanky new apartment across the road. A state-of-the-art gym to train at. Not to mention a nice new office for you, Carter. You get the privacy to do you here considering Noah, Declan, and now Oli have bought you the entire industrial estate."

"Andi," Shane said again and this time she looked at him.

"Just think about it, Carter." Andi was saying, a grin on her face. "It will be just like Manchester, only better. Nights in the pub. Building Rebel PR by attracting the future of the sports industry, music, and movies. You'll come home, move into the apartment, take over that offer me and Charlie had built for you and it will be fucking epic."

Turning to Eve, Andi said. "Shane knows all the right people to make you MMA's new shining star. Having him so near will be great. I promise you this is the best for everyone."

Shane didn't look convinced. In fact, he looked like he wanted to bolt out of the gym and get the hell out of Dodge. He looked at his watch again, and Eve was very tempted to tell him that if he checked his watch one more time, she'd shove it right up his ass.

The appeal of his looks was starting to be really fucked over by his piss-poor attitude.

"I mean, c'mon, Carter," Andi grinned, looking smug and it made Shane clench his jaw. "I'm handing you a golden ticket here. Free gaff. Fucking kick-ass clients. Hell, we can even spring for a pay rise, if you play hardball. But you won't, will ya? I even orchestrated the whole start of your best mate's love story like! It's a done deal. Right?"

Chapter Six

Shane

"I haven't agreed to anything yet."

"Technicalities. You know you can never say no to me. that's why you've been avoiding my calls for months."

"Don't fucking push me, Collins. I bloody mean it." Shane snarled at Andi, usually able to keep a check on his temper but dammit if Andi didn't drag it out of him.

"Um, do I not get a say in this? I mean Abercrombie here doesn't seem all that keen to manage me and like fuck I want someone who isn't interested in repping me." The MMA fighter, Eve tossed him a haughty look and Shane bristled.

It was obvious the woman had no clue who he was and that suited Shane. He'd waited for a sliver of recognition, and was only too delighted to not get any. If he wasn't so focused on his annoyance with Andi's railroading, then he'd be salivating at the chance to work with her. Andi knew that Shane had been trying to get an MMA fighter on his client list for ages and no one would expect him to be repping a girl who looked like she should be a fitness model rather than stepping foot in the octagon and kicking the shit out of other women.

Andi glared at Shane, then smiled at Eve. "He's interested. If I know Carter, and I do, he's annoyed at me for springing this on him. Shane is also probably seething that you didn't pop up on his radar so he could have convinced you to stay in the UK and avoid coming home here and having to spend time with me."

Eve glanced at Shane and then back at Andi. "Still, I signed with Rebel PR to get me in front of people who can help my career, Andi. I've been waiting ages for you to sort this and listen; I need a plan here. I'm not getting any younger and Abercrombie looks like he'd rather be anywhere else other than here."

"Stop calling me that." Shane found himself grumbling, hoping like hell the nickname didn't stick.

Eve just rolled her eyes and folded her arms across her chest. She pinned him with a stare that he knew was meant to intimidate him, but Shane wasn't that easily intimidated.

A wimp is what ya are, lad. a fucking sissy with a girl's illness.

His dad's voice was so loud in his head that Shane had to turn away and look around the gym. It was constantly there, his voice, but here, in Ireland, with the constant reminders of his failures, Shane was finding it harder to drown him out. He needed to work out, to run off his feelings, and get the hell out of this fucking country.

"Listen, I can assure you that Shane is the right person to manage you, Eve. I wouldn't have spent months convincing him that he needed to be here if he wasn't. Like I told you when you signed, I see massive things in your future and the person who can make that happen is Shane."

Andi's flattery never worked on Shane, even if his chest

did tighten a little at the conviction in her tone. He ran and through his hair, sighed, and took a little walk around the gym to assess whether it was worth his time or not. He tried to ignore the jerk in his heart when he spotted the gymnastics equipment in the farthest corner.

There was a beam, a pommel horse, bars, and above his head were the rings. He lifted his gaze and that longing he'd buried deep down came rushing back. God, he wanted to leap up and grip the rings and get that rush again, to feel invincible and like a superhero.

But he hadn't been invincible, had he?

Weak...you were fucking weak lad.

Shane closed his eyes and remembered the last interaction he had with his dad during a practice session, not long after the doctors cleared him to start working toward his comeback.

"It's too soon, dad. The doctor said I need a few more weeks before I attempt getting back on the rings."

His dad snorted. Shane knew the rings was his strongest apparatus. If he wanted to retain his European all-round title, he needed to get back to full strength. There was still a niggling in his shoulder. His doctor had told him that he was good to go, physically anyways.

Despite the couple of weeks in the retreat where he was given techniques to manage his bulimia, the moment he was home his dad went back to his usual demanding self and even started making sure that Shane ate with him so he could count the calories for him. Even when the phycologist told Henry to stop that pattern of behaviour because it was a trigger for Shane's obsession with food.

"Just get up there, your shoulder's grand. Or have you been up to your stupid little girl antics again and gonna make a fool of yourself, again."

Stupid little girl antics – that's what his dad had been

calling his bulimia, having not bothered to even acknowledge it, would probably have ignored it altogether if the Olympic council had not ordered an evaluation into Shane's mental health to make sure that the pressure of the games had not been detrimental to his mental health.

Shane had always known that he was nothing more than the medal he could win for his dad to brag about. That Shane the person didn't matter. It was Shane Carter, Olympian that was the cashpoint his dad wanted to look after. He was, what, eight weeks out of nearly killing himself for a medal and his dad hadn't even changed.

Shane was done. He couldn't do it anymore.

"I'm done, dad."

"For fuck sake, we've only started today and you're giving up already!"

Shane shook his head as he grabbed his tee. "No dad, all of it. Gymnastics, the Olympics. You. I'm done."

His dad looked at him and then laughed. "Like fuck you are. I fucking made you, lad. you won't embarrass me like this. As if it wasn't bad enough that you dropped like a stone on live TV, now you're throwing a tantrum. You got a dick between your legs, lad, or a fucking pussy? Cause you sure as shit are acting like a little bitch."

Shane wanted to punch him, he wanted to coil his fist up and smack him hard enough to feel bones break, but he stood there and absorbed what his dad was saying to him. Henry's eyes flicked to the tattoo on his left pectoral, and he smirked.

"You don't deserve to wear that tattoo. Only proper Olympians deserve to wear that tattoo and you sure as shit aren't a proper Olympian with a fucking first loser's medal. You make me sick. Maybe I have fucking bulimia too."

Pain pierced through Shane's skull at the memory. He'd walked out then and packed up his shit and checked into a hotel. He'd ordered a fuckton of room service, inhaling it all before he relapsed and puked it all up. It was Ronan who he had texted for help when his heart wouldn't stop racing and he'd not seen his dad since then.

"Shane?"

The sound of Andi's voice dragged him back to the present. Eve was looking at him with open curiosity and that was not a good thing. She seemed like the kind of woman who would ask a lot of questions and Shane didn't want to share the person he had been back then.

You're still a weak ass bitch, lad.

But Shane wanted to prove him wrong...he wanted to prove himself wrong.

"Listen, Andi," Eve started with a sigh. "He doesn't want the job. Hell, I'm not even sure he's up to the challenge. It's a lot different managing MMA and some fancy premier league footballer. Shit, he might look like he works out a lot, but I don't think it's a good fit. Find someone else."

Shane strode back over and pinned his eyes on the pint-sized fighter. "You're wrong. I've made careers for a lot of up-and-coming sports stars. Not just fancy footballers. I have contacts in every avenue, so I have what it takes to make you a superstar."

Eve snorted, and rolled her eyes. "Sure, you do, I bet Dana White is right there in your phone contacts."

Shane pulled out his phone, searched for the contact and held it up, for Eve to see, then he went into his photos and pulled up the picture of him sitting next to Conor McGregor at a fight a few years ago. Eve's mouth hung open and he saw a spark of fire in her eyes.

"Okay, hotshot, you got connections. Well done to you. But I need to know you can follow through on what you promise me. I need someone who knows what it's like to be an athlete. And despite the gym body, that's not you."

Andi opened her mouth, stopping when Shane held up

his hand. "I'm not an athlete, no, but my foot's already in most doors. Andi was right, I am the best person for the job. Let me prove it."

Chapter Seven

Shane

SHANE WASN'T sure what had possessed him to basically accept Andi's job there on the spot the other day, and yet here he was in his new apartment trying to arrange to have some of his stuff shipped over. The woman living across the hall from him, his new client, was also running circles in his mind after she'd just shrugged at him after his pitch.

"Andi was right, I am the best person for the job. Let me prove it."

Eve shrugged like she wasn't all that arsed about it all. "Okay, hotshot. Prove it and I might just keep you on. And if not, at least you're easy on the eyes, Abercrombie."

She'd sauntered away from him then, her firm ass on show in those tight shorts she was wearing. She looked over her shoulder, caught him looking, laughed, and then put the music on full blast and continued with her workout.

"Why didn't you tell her that you were an athlete before your injury?"

Shane snorted and lied his ass off. "It will make it all that more impressive when I get her on a big card. Don't tell her. Let me do what I told her I would. Let me prove it."

Andi had been just delighted and annoyingly smug, though when Shane told her that he could still manage Eve from Manchester, Andi had asked him to give Cork a go for at least a couple of months. She and Charlie had shown him his new apartment, and then he had gone to dinner with them, and it was like old times, except they were both engaged, and Charlie was pregnant.

He'd spent the entire day yesterday getting settled and considering he'd only brought one change of clothes with him; Shane had gone shopping for some other things to wear. It had felt weird walking around Cork City again. There was a time, as a teen, when he and Ronan couldn't walk down the street without women throwing themselves at both of them.

Hell, Ronan still had that problem but now he had a stunning blonde by his side who glared at them and the first time he had seen Sorcha Healy glare at a woman who was flirting with Ronan, he knew Ronan had found his person.

A knock sounded on his door and Shane stopped his sorting to go answer it. Ronan Cusack stood on the other side, his lips curving into a smile when Shane opened the door. Shane could see why women went mad when he smiled, but Shane also knew Ronan was one of the best people out there. He'd kept Shane's secrets for a long time, and he was one of the very few people that Shane trusted without question.

Ronan held up a bag. "I stopped by and grabbed some food for lunch. Didn't know if Andi had stocked you up before you moved in and I know you like some weird stuff in those salads of yours."

Shane laughed and headed back inside. "Hey, you joke but now you can't eat a salad without a little pineapple in it."

Ronan blushed, then shook his head. "Ya, but you don't have a fiancée who told everyone at a party about my little pineapple in salad quirk, and then said at least it was that and not finding out I was into the whole upside-down pineapple thing."

Shane looked at Ronan as he took a fresh pineapple out of the bag and looked at it.

"Apparently, it's a swingers thing," Ronan said as he opened the fridge and started to put the stuff in the fridge. "Which she explained to me in great detail. In front of every-one. It wouldn't have been a big deal but then Oli Scott and Sorcha started talking about sex terms and both Oli's fiancée and me were so red, we looked sunburned."

Shane barked out a laugh as Ronan's face heated again. "You chose to fall for a woman who has no filter, bud."

Ronan grinned and closed the fridge before putting some Nutri bars in the cupboard. "I did. And I regret nothing. Me and Niamh blamed the alcohol. No one believed us though. Tea?"

Ronan wiggled a box of Barry's Tea and Shane nodded. This felt normal. The two of them chatting and making tea. If anyone but Ronan had shown up with food Shane would have bristled and been pissed. However, this was Ronan, who knew all about Shane's disorder, and had gone shopping with Shane so many times that it felt normal.

"Where is your fiancée today?" Shane asked when Ronan came over with the cup of tea and they sat down.

Ronan took a sip of his tea, and then set it down on the coffee table. "Sorcha's at work but I am under strict orders to tell you that she expects you to come for dinner Saturday night and she wasn't going to take no for an answer.

Shane must have looked a little panicked, like he did when any plans for food were sprung on him and he couldn't pre-empt the menu, because Ronan leaned back in his seat.

"Don't worry. Sorcha is a terrible cook so I'll be cooking. Unless you want to order in and I can shoot you over the menus of some of the places we like to eat from near town. There's this Chinese who cooks clean rice and they have the most divine crispy chicken."

"Nicer that the place near your old place?" Shane asked, his panic fading as Ronan nodded. "Damn, that's high praise. Don't cook we can order in. Might as well get used to some of the stuff around here since I could be here a while."

Ronan leaned forward, Shane's friend obviously restless, his fingers tapping on the arm of the chair. "And how do you feel, now that you're back?"

Shane took a gulp of tea, then leaned back in his chair, and rested a leg over the other. "Weird. Strange. It almost feels like I never left, but also that I've been away for a long time. I hate that Andi forced my hand. I hate that she put me in this position, and then I hate myself because if she knew what being here makes me feel, I know she'd let me go."

"Maybe you should tell her that, if it gets too much."

Shane sighed, running a hand through his hair. "I really hope it doesn't come to that. I'd hate for her and Charlie to start treating me like I'm breakable. It helps knowing that Henry isn't in Cork right now."

A muscle in Ronan's cheek twitched. His friend had made it no secret that he wasn't Henry Carter's biggest fan, Ronan's loyalty to Shane unbreakable. He remembered when his dad had showed up at Shane's hotel room, and Ronan had lost his temper, shouting at his dad to just fuck off and leave Shane alone, then slamming the door in Henry's face.

"And where is Henry these days?"

Shane had made sure to figure out where his dad was so there was no chance that their paths might cross while Shane was in Cork. His dad still had active social media accounts for Shane to nose at, and make sure that his dad wasn't making any more kids miserable.

"Dublin, apparently. He got some job with Gymnastics Ireland. He posts photos all the time."

Ronan's face was impassive as he said. "It would only take a couple of calls, Shane. Couple of calls and the bastard would never work in gymnastics again. Just say the word and I can get it done."

Shane's best friend was one of the nicest people in the goddamn world and if he was ready to do some underhand shit for Shane, that told him all he needed to know about the other man.

Shane laughed, shaking his head. "The job isn't with kids, if it was, I'd have said something long ago. Apart from being a grade A prick, Henry was good at getting sponsorship and deals. He made me enough money before I was eighteen to leave him and all his shit. But I appreciate your offer of vengeance and I love ya for it."

Ronan inclined his head, then asked Shane with a grin. "Do ya love me enough to be my best man?"

Ronan had been in a fake relationship with Sorcha before they had fallen in love, and after only a couple of months, had come back in the new year with Sorcha sporting a massive red rock on her engagement finger.

Shane blinked, surprised even as delight flushed through his veins. "Me?"

Ronan rolled his eyes. "Like I'd have anyone else. You're my brother, Shane. I'd be honoured to have you stand beside me when I marry the woman I love."

Shane got to his feet and so did Ronan. He walked over to his friend, and they embraced. Shane answered Ronan's question as they did. "It would be my honour, Ro. My absolute fucking honour."

Chapter Eight

Eve

A COUPLE of days had passed since meeting her new manager and apart from a few emails about deals he was working on, Eve hadn't seen Mr. Abercrombie except for seeing him heading over to Rebel PR, or going out with Ronan Cusack, Hollywood's latest sweetheart, who according to Andi, was Shane's best mate.

He'd asked her to send him over a detailed outline of her training and dietary needs, so that he could be on top of any specific requirements, and it had irked her. The bluntness of the emails, though professional, was a new thing for Eve. She wasn't used to having someone rigidly checking up on her to make sure she was doing what she already knew she had to be doing to be fight ready.

Eve had ignored the email until she got a text from Andi with a video of Shane in his office, sitting on his chair with his feet on the desk, throwing an American Football up and down, a cocky smile on his face as Eve heard him say something that made her skin pebble.

"Come on, Mandy. It's one sparring session. Come to Ireland, spar with my girl, we take a few photos, shoot a few reels, and you get some promo for your next throwdown. You know you can't say no to me."

Andi angled the camera as Eve heard a laugh, and a maybe as Amanda Fucking Nunes rolled her eyes at Shane.

What in the actual fuck was happening right now?

How the fuck did the model know fucking Amanda Nunes.

Another text came through that just said: Answer his damn emails.

Eve had immediately taken out her laptop and attached her training schedule, her food intake, and what she was missing at the gym to be able to train properly. She got a response a few minutes later thanking her and he would work on things. Then another line that said he'd meet with her Monday afternoon at the gym to go through his progress.

Too amped up to do anything else, Eve had headed into town to grab a few bits at a local sports store, then headed over to Rebel Ink to check in with her cousin, Darren. He was one of her favourite people in the world and he'd been through the ringer a couple of times.

His parents hadn't wanted a kid to ruin their lifestyle, so they had dumped Darren on his grandmother, which was a blessing in disguise. She'd raised Darren as her own and encouraged his flare for art. School hadn't been his thing and she'd allowed him to jack it in to pursue a career in tattooing.

It was under the previous owner's tutelage that Darren had found an extended family. His Rebek Ink family had been there for him through thick and thin, and he them, and Eve had been delighted to see him so happy and contented.

Then his beloved gran had died, and it had hit Darren hard. It didn't help his parents were being massive dickheads about it all. He hadn't told her what he was going through, how dark it got for him, but then he fell in love with a woman who had been the victim of an abusive relationship and terrified of her own shadow.

Nessa Kennedy was a stronger woman than anyone knew, but Darren has seen it. Even when her sicko Ex had taken Nessa and a few others hostage, Darren had ridden to the rescue and made her so fucking proud of him.

That had all happened last year, and they were still all loved up and shit. Nessa was still shy around her and had been surprised when Eve had offered to teach her a few self-defence moves. Darren told Eve that he'd already offered, but Eve had snorted, telling Nessa that girls fought smarter than boys, so Eve was happy to show her how to throw a punch if she wanted.

Nessa hadn't been sure, but she had thanked Eve for the offer, then agreed to come watch her spar with Quinn, when she was next back in Cork during her next week or so off from being a legend in F1.

Eve pushed open the door of Rebel Ink, grinned as she heard the heavy hip hop beats and knew her cousin was working. Having spent a lot of time here whenever she was back in the country, she knew that both Cathal and Darren leaned toward more hip-hop beats, while Isaac Jacobs the other merry musketeer liked indie and grunge.

Shay Gleeson liked rock and indie, with a little bit of metal thrown in so it was like having a mixtape on in the shop when they were all together. Eve looked over at the wall and laughed out loud when she read a sign that said shop rules.

1. No crying. You're paying for this shit so suck it up.

2. Don't be the smelly guy we talk about for years after you get tattooed.

3. We have the right to eject you for being an asshole. So don't be one.

4. The music is at the discretion of the artist. We aren't a

radio station, and we don't take requests. There will be no Nickelback, no T-swift, no Bieber, or any other generic shite.

5. Pricing is final. We don't haggle. Save that for your next holiday in Spain or whatever.

There were a few more, but a stunning young woman Eve hadn't met before came out and asked Eve if she was okay. The woman was a little younger than Eve and had a doe eyed kinda face and big brown eyes.

"I'm here to see, Fitz. I'm Eve."

"Rylee. He's in the back having lunch before his next client. Head on back."

Eve strode through the shop, pausing to lean against the door of Cathal Horgan's room where the man was working on a design, and he lifted his handsome face to where Eve was standing. She'd had a thing for Cathal for ages, but the man was with a genuine rockstar and all loved up. That didn't stop her from messing with him.

"Hey handsome. I'm ready to get naked for my tattoo."

Cathal shook his head, rolling his eyes though there was a smile on his lips. "Fuck right off, Eve. Fitz is out back."

She pouted at him, which caused him to laugh, and then he went back to his design.

Eve strode into the kitchen as Darren filled a cup of coffee for her, then sat back down and munched on his gigantic sandwich. She sat across from him, blew on the coffee and then took a sip.

"Luna would stab you with a drumstick for flirting with her man."

Eve had met Luna once, and she was a good laugh. Eve had been upfront that she'd had a thing for Cathal ages ago, and Luna had patted Cathal's chest and told Eve that Cathal was all hers now, she could look but not touch.

Eve had immediately liked the other woman.

"Luna has given me her full permission to admire the goods but not to touch them. We have an understanding."

Darren chuckled, then asked her how things were doing with her new manager. Eve told him about the emails, the way he had looked the day they had met, and how she was started to rethink signing with Rebel PR. It was grand to have Darren to get her reservations off her chest, cause her cousin didn't bullshit.

"This is a big deal for you, cuz," Darren started, taking a drink of his Coke. "I get that, but Andi knows her shit. She's not gonna waste your talent if this Shane fella if he wasn't good. Give him a chance and look, I know it's a family fucking trait and all, but try and have patience. He seems to have hit the ground running sending you all the deals on offer and letting you choose what works for you. Like, just remember your fave cousin when you headline a UFC card and give me tickets."

Eve tapped her chin with her finger. "I think I'd give your ticket to sexy boss man in the next room. At least he'd still look pretty through a swollen eye."

Darren clutched at his chest like he was offended, then scoffed the remainder of his sandwich before chugging back his drink. He got to his feet and looked at Eve. "As I said, give him a chance and if it still doesn't feel right, then talk to Andi. If it's not gonna work, she'll understand. Andi's good peeps."

Her cousin went back to work, giving her a kiss on the top of her head before asking her to hang around and come to dinner with him and Nessa when she finished her shift across the road. Eve did just that because it wasn't like it was a hardship to hang around and watch Cathal for the afternoon.

No hardship at all.

CHAPTER NINE

Eve

BY THE TIME Monday came around, Eve had decided to do exactly what Darren had said and give both Andi, and by default, Shane, a chance to prove they had her best interests at heart. Knowing she had a meeting later with Shane, she'd gone to the gym to try and rid herself of the anxious tension in her and was delighted when Noah was there.

They'd become sort of friends over the last while and when he came out of the office to ask Eve if she wanted to spar with the new pads Shane had gotten her, it had made her grin to see Noah bring out the kickboxing pads. Abercrombie had pulled something out of the bag at least.

When Eve asked him what was wrong with his face because he was frowning so hard, he told her Charlie had a doctor's appointment this afternoon and it would be the last one he could attend with her cause he was leaving next week for the new season. Eve could tell he was stressed.

Stripping off her hoodie and her tracksuit bottoms, she wore just a camo top and skintight leggings. She took off her trainers and then strapped her feet. Eve needed to feel every kick, every vibration to know whether the hit was good, or her angle was right. There was a boxing ring in the centre of the gym, not as wide as an MMA ring, but it would do in principle.

It was the first time she missed being in Liverpool. She missed having an Octagon on hand to practice in and people there who understood her and her process. Noah Donovan was a perfect specimen of an athlete, but his process was different to hers. She needed to take in a hell of a lot of calories to maintain her training and keep her energy levels right.

She'd sat down with Noah and Quinn, who deferred to her boyfriend and race manager because as she said, she couldn't cook for shit. Eve had learned little bits over the years, enough to get by, and yet, it was strange to hear all of their little quirks when it came to eating.

Eve had asked Quinn if she had cheat days and the petite racer had clamped her mouth shut and Oskar had chuckled, telling Eve that when he had met Quinn, she was on a first name basis with at least six different food delivery drivers and gets whiney if she goes too long without chips and curry.

Noah called her over to help him strap on the pads when she had warmed up a little. Eve asked Noah if he minded if they turned on a little music because Eve trained to block out the noise of the crowd during a fight. Her sparring partner just nodded as Eve pressed play and Yonaka's *Teach Me to Fight* roared on the speakers.

Noah tapped the pads together and it was go time. Eve practiced some of her punch and kick combos, Noah doing a great job at shouting moves at her. One of the weird things about her body was her arms might be short, meaning a closer contact fight in her upper body, but her legs were long. She sometimes used her kick to keep her opponent at bay.

Her trainers in Liverpool called her fighting scrappy. They told her that women were afraid to fight her because while a lot of fighters used the same moves over and over again meaning they were an easy study, Eve adapted her fighting style depending on her opponent. If someone didn't like close combat, Eve made sure there was no breathing space between them. If someone liked to dance around the octagon to tire out their opponent, Eve stood still and bounced on her feet, getting the crowd going.

Eve spent the next hour or so kicking the pads and releasing some of the tension that had been building in her over the last week. Running only calmed her a little, but this, feeling the burn in her thighs and calves from kicking, the sting on the front of her foot, it made her feel so fucking alive it was insane.

When Noah shouted over the music a little while later and called time, Eve's skin was slick with sweat and her lungs burned, though it was in the best possible way. Noah slipped his hands out of the pads, went to the corner of the ring and grabbed their water bottles, handing one over to Eve and she opened it and threw some of it over her face.

"Damn, I fucking needed that."

"You okay?" Noah asked, concern on his face.

"Ah, I'm grand," Eve told him, slightly amused that the stoic driver would be concerned for her. But then again, Eve had seen how he was with Quinn, with Luke Sullivan, his former teammate, and even with Andi, though they pretended to dislike one another.

Noah was gonna make a great dad, Eve was sure of it.

She grabbed the remote and turned off the music before turning back to answer Noah. "I get a little angsty when I've not had a fight in a while. Probably the same for you with driving. That rush. That buzz is unlike anything else."

Noah smiled as he nodded. "Ya, fuck, I get it. It's like a

drug. Though getting punched in the face for a living seems a little more..."

His words trailed off and Eve laughed. "Sadistic? Mental? Crazy? Ya, I get told that a lot. But taking a crash at 5Gs amounts to the same thing."

"Not when you've only crashed once in your entire career." Noah snorted, then looked at the clock. "Shit, I gotta go meet Charlie for her doctor's appointment. But if you still need to beat someone up, you can beat up Shane."

Noah ducked out of the ring as Eve turned to see Shane walking in with Andi's fiancé Declan Walsh. Declan was the lead singer of Heartache Melody and was a sexy son of a bitch even when he wasn't singing with that voice of his. He and Shane, who was holding his own next to the rockstar in the sexiness department, were lost in conversation until Noah passed them. Then Declan walked out with Noah.

Damn, she really needed to get laid...

Shane came toward her, and kicked off his trainers before ducking into the ring. Eve watched with curiosity as he planted his feet on the floor and bounced a little like he was testing the floor. When he lifted his gaze to see Eve watching him, he looked a little sheepish, like she had caught him out on something.

Interesting.

"Making good use of the pads I see."

Jesus, the sound of his voice made her suppress a shiver. She really did need to get laid if the sound of his voice made her want to ride him.

Shane cleared his throat and Eve realized that she'd been staring at him. Tossing her water bottle to the side, Eve folded her arms across her chest. "Ya thanks for those. What about the other stuff on my list. And I'll need a new sparring partner since Noah and Quinn are leaving soon. Have ya sorted that yet?"

A muscle ticked in his jaw. "The equipment you asked for has been ordered and I'm working to try and get you a couple of hours a week in one of the Cork MMA gyms. There's some...politics I have to navigate through but I'm getting there. And you don't need a new sparing partner. Use me."

Eve wanted to shove him down on the mat and use him alright.

Pushing those thoughts out of her head, Eve snorted. "I wouldn't want to break that pretty boy face, Abercrombie."

"Stop calling me that." Shane muttered.

They stared at each other, locked in a silent battle of wills until Shane sighed. "C'mon, Eve. You obviously don't think I'm good enough to spar with you or I don't know how to best utilise your skills. You assume I don't know what it's like to be in your shoes, so show me."

"What?" Eve said with a snort, rolling her eyes. "So, you want me to what, punch you?"

Shane shrugged. "If that's what it fucking takes, then ya, hit me."

"I'm not gonna fucking deck ya, Abercrombie."

"I told you to stop calling me that," Shane growled at her, and it heated her body way more than she wanted it to.

Eve didn't say anything and just stared at Shane as he arched a brow in a silent challenge before he spoke again. "Do it." His tone taunted Eve, as his lips curved into a smug smile.

Fucking men. Typical fucking men. They thought they knew everything.

Idiots the lot of them.

She wasn't used to backing down from anyone, least of all a man who was too good-looking for his own good, and too fucking smug for her to stand it.

Eve coiled her arm back, clenched her fist, and then shrugged. "Alright," Eve said, and then hit him right in the face without holding back.

Chapter Ten

Shane

Fucking hell this girl could punch.

Maybe he was a masochist, or maybe just a sucker for pain, but no sane man would invite a woman who broke people's faces for a living to punch him. And yet, that was exactly what Shane had done when Eve had appeared that she was looking down her nose at him.

He'd been bloody triggered by it and now, he was just fucking bloody, and his face felt like he'd been hit by a two-by-four, and how the hell had he ended up on his ass on the mat?

Shane swung his legs, working to gather enough momentum to land his dismount cleanly on the horizontal bars. It was one of his weakest apparatuses, so he wanted to practice over and over until his routine was clean enough that he felt comfortable with it.

He was a little shorter in the legs than most of the boys who made this apparatus look so easy, but his dad was hoping that he'd get a growth spurt over the summer break and come back taller. Shane wasn't looking forward to the time when he might grow a few inches or add some bulk to his frame. He'd have to adjust his entire repertoire to accommodate any changes to his body and that meant his dad would be on his case even more than he was.

Ronan had asked him to go to the cinema with him the weekend and his dad told him that he didn't have time for frivolous teenage crap when being the first Irish gold medal Olympian was on the cards. Shane wanted to be a normal teenager for one weekend, where he wasn't consumed with training and dieting or studying old videos to improve his own routines.

Shane dismounted from the bar, and he nearly cheered and pumped his fists when he stuck the landing. Henry Carter didn't believe in celebrating when it wasn't in front of the camera, and he certainly didn't give his son any praise.

"Your legs were parted on the second swing set. And you over-rotated on the crossovers. Do it again."

No. Shane was wrecked. His muscles ached and he was fucking starving. His dad had kept him in the training centre since after lunch and it was well past eight now. He wanted to shower and go to bed and maybe play some video games with Ronan. He was too tired to do it all again and knew he wouldn't do the routine any better without some rest.

But his dad thought he knew more about Shane's body than he did.

"Not tonight, dad. I'm tired."

Henry glared at him. "Stop whining and do as you're told, lad. You stop when I see you've done what I told ya to do. Not before."

Shane was so damn tired that his mouth moved before he could stop himself. "If you think you can do a better job, then you can fucking give it a go yourself."

His dad looked at him for a split second before his hand lashed out. He hit Shane right in the nose with his clenched fist. Shane heard bone crunch and pain splintered across his face as he went down. More blood poured from his nose as Shane lifted his hand to his nose and then down and saw all the blood on his hand.

His dad had hit him. His dad had broken his nose.

Panic flared in his dad's eyes as he reached for Shane and Shane scampered back, recoiling in case his dad hit him again. His dad berated him, and shouted at him, he might grab Shane or push him around, but he'd never once hit him.

Until today.

"You shouldn't have backchatted, lad."

So, Shane was taking the blame for this. Right okay. He was used to that. That was nothing new. It was always his fault. It was Shane's fault his mam had left, it was Shane's fault that Henry was a single dad, it was Shane's fault when he was too tired to go to school because Henry had kept him in the gym working on his routines till stupid o'clock in the morning.

When the door to the office in the centre opened, Henry shouted for someone to come and help Shane, that he had fallen off the bar and landed on his face. Shane locked eyes with his dad, and it was there, in his eyes, ordering Shane to fall in line and stick to the story.

Shane had no other choice, did he? He lied to the medic, to the doctor in the hospital, and to the nurse who checked him over and frowned at the bruises and other things on his body, his dad saying that it was all from hard work because his son was going to be an Olympian one day.

The doctor told him to rest up for three weeks to allow his nose to heal.

His dad had him training again the following morning.

And that was how Shane learned to perform through the pain.

"Hey, fuck, are you okay? You did ask me to punch you."

He had, hadn't he?

Shane groaned as he rolled to his side and tried to get to his feet. He got to one knee before his vision swam and his nose dripped blood onto the mat. His stomach rolled and he had to fight the urge not to upchuck on the floor. The ringing in his ears indicated that with one punch, this tiny, beautiful girl might have given him a concussion.

No fucking wonder Shane was having trouble getting anyone to fight her.

They were afraid of her.

His ears were still ringing when he felt arms hoist him into an upright position and then hands gripped his shoulders to keep him standing. Shane blinked to clear the haze in his vision and made out that Declan was the one holding him up.

"Hey mate, you okay? She clocked you nice and good."

Shane swallowed hard, and tasted blood in his throat. "I'm okay. I don't think she broke my nose. I know what that feels like, and it doesn't feel broken."

Declan chuckled. "Brave man asking a brawler to deck ya one. Christ, I can't even tell if you're bruised with all the blood. Let me grab you a clean tee and you can go clean up in the bathroom."

"I'm alright."

A hand squeezed his shoulder. "Andi would rip my balls off if I didn't look after you. Gimmie a second."

Shane braced himself on the buckle and closed his eyes. The blood was gushing from his nose, so Shane whipped off his tee and held it to his nose to try and stem the bleeding.

"Jesus, I'm so fucking sorry. Are you okay?"

Shane turned to look at Eve, who to be fair looked like she was about to get sick.

"I'm grand. Believe it or not, my face has been hit harder before. My body can take it."

Eve's gaze dipped, and had he not been bleeding profusely all over the gaff, then he might have thought she was checking him out. Her eyes were laser-focused on his chest and then it dawned on Shane that she was staring at the tattoo on his pec, the Olympic rings.

"What's that?" she asked him as Declan came out with a black tee.

"Nothing. Absolutely fucking nothing. I'm gonna go clean up."

Shane ducked under the ropes as Declan held them apart for him and he made his escape to the bathroom beside the office. He shoved tissue up his nose and washed the blood from his face and hands. He braced his hands on the side of the sink and looked at himself in the mirror.

Wimp. Sissy boy. Letting a girl knock you on your ass. You never did grow a pair of balls, did ya, lad? Always weak. Always a failure. A fucking disappointment. No wonder your mam ran off with a weak-ass little bitch of a son like you.

The nausea that had been sloshing around in his stomach had enough. Shane leaned forward and vomited up the contents of his stomach. He'd learned long ago how to vomit in silence, and he just let his body take over and to purge the meagre meals he'd had that day.

When his body resorted to empty reaching, Shane took a few deep breaths to calm himself down. he lifted his gaze to look at himself in the mirror. He hated how he felt after getting sick. He felt in control, accomplished, like this was some big fucking achievement and not that he was teetering on a slippery slope that he might not come back from this time.

His heart was pounding in his chest and Shane told himself it was from getting punched. He pulled the tee Declan had given him on, wiped his mouth with the back of his hand, reached into his pocket, and took out a mint, a habit he'd gained along with the bulimia.

This didn't count as a relapse. He hadn't made himself sick. That was all Eve and her killer right hook. He was in control. He was in the driver's seat. There was nothing to worry about.

Right?

CHAPTER ELEVEN

Shane

SHANE THREW himself into work to distract himself from the craving he was drowning in to feel the same things he had felt in the gym's bathroom. He'd deviated from his routine over the course of the week, and he wasn't proud of how close he was to walking over to the cupboard and taking out his secret stash of junk found and binging until he made himself sick.

His head told him he needed to call his psychologist, get an appointment, or hell, pick up the phone and call Ronan for help. But his best friend was back in the UK to do a first run-through of the TV series he was gonna be filming with Joshua "JJ" James, and it was a big deal. Ronan would drop everything to come and sit with him and Ronan had done that too many times before.

Two years.

That was how long between when they had diagnosed him with bulimia, and his first proper relapse since he'd made a conscious effort to start the road to recovery. His new life in

Manchester had been refreshing. He loved the anonymity that he had. No one knew who he was, what he used to be, and he felt like he could breathe.

But that all changed yesterday.

They'd been in class, messing about like they always did, Andi Collins the main instigator. He'd never expected to find friends like the girls who were from Cork. They were a year older than him and had been city girls when he was from West Cork, so they hadn't run in the same circles. They themselves hadn't met until first year in Manchester so it was a running joke between them all.

Garret Langston barrelled into the glass and went right to the projector up the front. "You guys, you are not gonna guess what I found out this weekend. Someone's been hiding a massive fucking secret."

They all looked at one another and Shane tried not to think that it might have been him who had been found out. Everyone knew Charlie was the daughter of a Formula 1 tycoon, and Andi was the sister of one of the lads in the Irish band that was starting to get noticed. He pleaded with whatever god or gods were in the universe that it wasn't about him.

Shane's heart sank when he watched himself appear on the screen and everyone turned to stare at him. panic started to make his heart race as Garret shouted for everyone to watch.

It was a sizzle reel of his career. From his first gymnastics competition at age five to European and Olympic trials. He felt sick to his stomach as his classmates oohed and aaahed at the moves he was doing onscreen. Andi looked at him when there was a picture of him standing beside Simone Biles at some competition and they were both laughing.

Shane got to his feet when Olympic footage started to play, and he knew what was gonna happen. They were going to show the fall and Shane would have to watch it again. It had already been burned into his memory because his dad had made him watch it over and over, so Shane would see how much he had fucked up.

"Turn it off," Shane said but no one was listening to him. Andi and Charlie were watching him, concern on their faces as Shane beat a fist on the desk in front of him, his anger and fear making him act in a way he hardly ever did.

"Turn it fucking off."

"Do it, Garrett," Andi ordered and Garret paused it at the moment when he stuck a landing on the floor and the snapshot of his face when Shane had realized that he was guaranteed a silver medal at the least made present-day Shane yearn for the sport he had walked away from so he would live.

How could someone have not known that he was suffering? He could see the pain on his face, even through the triumph. He could feel the burn in his shoulder now, even though it had long since healed. He could have returned to gymnastics. He had made the choice not to.

"Kept that fucking quiet, Carter. Ladies and gentlemen, we've got an Olympian in our midst."

Shane grabbed his things and fled the room as Andi called after him. No. He couldn't face them and all the questions. Everyone would find out soon enough that he'd made a fool of himself by falling on his face on worldwide TV.

He didn't stop until he was back in his apartment. He didn't stop until he pulled the travel suitcase from under his bed and shovelled the contents of it into his mouth, devouring the chocolate and crisps like he hadn't eaten in months.

For a moment, that split second, the high made him sit there and close his eyes. Then he was bolting to the bathroom and puking his guts out. Even when he felt like he had nothing left in his stomach, Shane shoved his fingers down his throat and made himself vomit more.

His heart was pounding, and he felt like he was dying. The doctors had told him this could happen, it was a heart *arrhythmia brought on by the purging. Shane pulled out his phone and sent a text to Ronan.*

His friend had a key, so about a half hour later, as Shane was still sat on the bathroom floor, resting his head against the cold wall, Ronan appeared in the doorway.

"Shane. What happened?"

"They all know. They all know about me." Shane told him and he felt so ashamed that tears slipped from his eyes.

Ronan got down on the ground with him, slung his arm around his shoulder, and pulled Shane to him. "It's okay. I got you. I'm here."

Shane had always been grateful to have Ronan in his life and Shane had repaid the favour when his skanky ex had cheated on him and Ronan had gotten drunk and done some very un-Ronan-like things. After a year or two of jobs drying up, it was Shane who had told him to have a chat with Andi about signing with Rebel PR, and that she was the best person to handle his acting career.

His stomach rumbled and Shane glanced at his watch. It was after three in the afternoon, and he'd not eaten since, well, since the dinner he'd eaten last night with Andi while they discussed things for Eve. He'd played with the pasta, eating when he caught Andi watching him.

So, Shane had eaten the food and drank his beer and felt shitty while doing it.

It had taken all his self-control when he crossed the road to his apartment not to go right into the bathroom and force himself to be sick. Shane had gone to bed at like nine to try and stop himself and this morning when he'd woken at five, he just couldn't bring himself to eat anything.

His stomach had rumbled this morning and yet, he'd felt too full. He'd gone to the gym knowing no one else would be there, especially not Eve, who had been avoiding him mostly since the whole punch thing. His nose felt much better, and the bruising was starting to fade, so there was no need to be avoiding him.

She'd even been edgy when he'd stopped by during the week to watch her train and tell her about the brand that he wanted her to think about letting sponsor her. Shane had done his research and he noticed that Eve liked to pay her dues and support her own. There was this up-and-coming sports brand that Shane had felt would be perfect for her and they were eager to get Eve on their books, as it would catapult their profile. Andi had agreed with the pairing and wanted to set up a photoshoot to get Eve's picture and presence out there.

Eve had taken a little persuading, skeptical about looking like a model and not a fighter, however, Shane had been able to talk her round. She'd had a video call with the clothing brand to talk about what she liked in fitness clothing, and they would bring the outfits to the shoot next week.

Until then, Shane would work behind the scenes and lock down the televised fight that he had almost bagged for Eve. He'd not tell her till it was certain, though. Until the contract was in his inbox and ready for her to sign.

His stomach rumbled again, a twist of pain in his stomach as Shane found himself walking toward the drawer that he really shouldn't be going anywhere near. Pulling open the drawer, his eyes latched onto the very organized chocolate and junk food he'd bought on a whim the day after he'd been punched.

Shane knew he should walk away and go ask for help, for a distraction and yet, he was hungry though and one small bar of dairy milk wouldn't do him any harm...right?

Chapter Twelve

Eve

Eve hadn't been sure about throwing her lot in with a new brand that wanted to sponsor her, especially when bigger brands had offered more money for her to exclusively wear their clothes. It had been Shane who had sold the brand to her.

"Think about it, Eve. The hometown hero deciding to wear a brand that no one else is wearing who just happens to be from Ireland. Turning down the massive brands because everyone else is wearing them, that's ballsy. And when you wear their gear in the ring, to training, and others follow you, everyone will know Eve did it first."

Eve snorted and toyed with the end of her ponytail. "You should sell holiday homes, Abercrombie. Or used cars. Either would work with a pitch like that."

Shane had laughed at her then, and she had smiled back, looking too long into his brown eyes before she looked away. She'd noticed he looked tired though, and she didn't want him killing himself to prove himself to her.

They'd agreed to hold the photo shoot at the gym so at least she didn't feel any more anxious than she already did. Eve wasn't used to doing all this girlie shite and having people take her photo. Andi was here too, talking to the clothing brand's manager so Eve busied herself with looking through the gear.

They'd listened to her and gone for the colours that she liked to wear, greens, blues, greys, and black. No pink or yellow which made her look stupid. She saw some really cool gear she could see herself wearing when she fought, the designer having told her that the material was designed to be sweat-resistant, and lightweight, and breathable.

Right now, Eve was wearing a grey sports bra and a pair of matching shorts. They fit her like a second skin. Eve did a couple of moves to see if she could move in them, and to her pleasant surprise she could. She did a kick and almost smacked her foot into Shane's chest.

He had her ankle caught in his grasp, a strange expression on his face, and by hell if the contact didn't sizzle. Shane dropped her leg, then broke the eye contact to look at the clothes.

"You like what you see?"

Eve dipped her gaze to the firm globes of his ass. "Uh-huh"

Shane started to turn back to look at her and she quickly snapped her gaze back up and at the clothes. Her face felt flushed, and Shane gave her an amused look, before sifting through the hangers on the rail.

"I can't believe they knocked all this up in a week. Like we only spoke on that call, and I'd wear every single thing hanging there." Eve told him, walking over to stand beside him.

"They want to impress you," Shane said, and Eve saw a faint smile on his lips. "You could have gone with the other deals. Most would have. It's a hell of a lot of money to turn down but I told Andi when I gave your answer that you weren't the kind of girl who cared about the money. You love the thrill of fighting and you'd never be content to take time out for a brand that wasn't solely focused on you."

Eve looked sideways at him. "You learned all that from the couple of weeks you've spent watching me?"

Shane shrugged. "I'm good at my job, Eve. I listen and I observe. I've seen the type of clothes you wear and knew this would be the right fit. It's the first of many deals. I have lots more up my sleeve for you."

Eve opened her mouth to retort, but someone called her name and asked if she was ready to get started. Shane helped her put on the boxing gloves for the first part of the shoot, then helped her into the ring by sitting on the ropes so she could duck inside. He stayed on the outside, calling her back to tighten the Velcro on her wrists.

"Make sure not to deck the photographer when she asks you to pretend to punch the camera. That costs a hell of a lot more than my nose." Shane teased her and her mouth parted. This was a side of him she hadn't seen before, and Eve was starting to think that there was more to Shane Carter than the man himself let on.

Eve laughed and mock-punched him on the arm. The photographer was asking her assistant to adjust the lighting and then she lifted her head and let out a gasp that had Eve focusing on the woman. Eve knew that Andi had asked her because she was young and new and eager to help out Rebel PR. And she must be good, or both the clothing brand and Andi wouldn't have hired her.

But the woman's focus wasn't on Eve...no...she was looking at Shane like Oli fucking Scott had walked in here balls ass naked. Like, Eve couldn't blame her for thinking he was hot, because as much as she hated to admit it, Eve was attracted to him too.

"Oh my god, it is you!" The photographer was saying, her

cheeks pink. "I saw the name and was like, it couldn't be him. oh my god, I'm totally fangirling right now."

The entire gym was watching the interaction. Eve glanced at Shane, who was wearing a tight smile as he leaned into the ring and held out his hand. "Shane Carter, nice to meet you."

"Oh my god, I know who you are. I mean, God, I'm stuttering."

Shane laughed and kept his hand out until the photographer shook it. He looked like he'd rather be anywhere but here right now, and Eve was confused as all hell as to what was going on.

"I'm a massive fan. I mean, I was. I had your poster on my wall growing up and that picture of you that was in that fitness magazine made me want to be a photographer. I sound like such a stalker."

Ya, she fucking did…when the hell was Abercrombie in a fitness magazine? Like as a model?

Shane chuckled, then ran his hand through his hair. "It's grand. I'm flattered."

The photographer looked at Eve and then back at Shane. "Look, this is crazy, and I never thought I'd have an opportunity like this, but would you take a few pictures with Eve?"

Eve watched as Shane's face went blank. "This is Eve's shoot, and I don't pose for photos anymore. Different life. I'm happier behind the camera. Today's all about Eve."

The woman looked disappointed, and her face fell. She opened her mouth to try and convince Shane, but he'd already jumped down from the ring and strode over to Andi. He stood there, his jaw clenched, and his arms folded across his chest. Andi leaned in and said something to him, and he just nodded sharply, and Andi turned back to focus on the shoot.

Once the photographer had composed herself, and she had stopped drooling over Shane, Eve marvelled at how good she was. It didn't feel like a photoshoot, and Eve enjoyed herself despite the niggling feeling that she was missing something important.

A couple of hours later and lots of outfit changes and Eve was done. She thanked everyone and the designer, chatted to them as they packed up, and then went to throw on her joggers. Andi came over and congratulated her, telling her that she might try and get the photographer to do a shoot with some of the Rebel PR clients for a promo shoot.

"What was that with Abercrombie?" Eve asked and Andi looked over to where the woman was asking Shane to sign something.

"You don't know?" Andi said, sounding very amused.

"Know what? Jesus, what the fuck don't I know?"

Andi grinned as they both watched Shane pose for a selfie with the woman. "Shane Carter is a bona fide Olympian. Has the medals in all to prove it. Such a shame he fucked up his shoulder and couldn't compete anymore. He was something special."

The goddamn tattoo...it was the Olympic rings right there on his chest and she'd missed it.

Abercrombie was a fucking Olympic medal-winning athlete and Eve cringed thinking back how she tossed at him that he hadn't a clue about being an athlete. As if he felt her eyes on him, Shane looked over his shoulder for a hot second before he looked away.

"What was his discipline?"

"Gymnastics," Andi said and Eve's stomach sank. "Don't tell him I told you. Maybe now you'll believe me when I tell you Shane has got you. shit, I better go rescue him before he stops pretending to be nice. He hates this crap."

Andi rushed off, leaving Eve to pull on her hoodie. She sat down on the bench and took a drink from her water bottle, her curiosity itching for her to google the man who was responsible for her career. This sort of changed things, right?

Shane knew what it was like to reach the pinnacle of success. Her career was safe in his hands, Eve was sure of it.

But Shane had hid his previous career from her, kept it a secret. Eve couldn't help but wonder what other secrets was Shane Carter hiding.

Chapter Thirteen

Shane

"THE SHOOT WENT WELL," Andi was saying to him as she was sat across the way from him. "The photos your fangirl sent on look amazing. Eve looks fucking sensational."

Shane dragged his eyes away from the email that had just landed in his inbox and looked at Andi with a come-on expression. Of course, she ignored him and scrolled through her phone. He'd gotten the same photos that Andi had and there was no denying that Eve was off the charts sexy, especially in those black and grey shots. There was this one photo, where she was striking a pose and someone had made her laugh, and the photographer had captured it, that Shane had stared at for far too long.

He had to stop thinking about how it would feel to make her laugh, because he couldn't go there. Not only was Eve his client, and it would be unprofessional, but Shane hadn't been in a relationship for longer than a few weeks because the moment it started to get serious, he withdrew because he was afraid that his girlfriends would find out his secret.

Eve knowing his secret was a bad idea. She'd tell Andi and Andi would tell Charlie and it would get out. The truth about his Olympic fall and the fact his dad had hidden his eating disorder and forced Shane to do the same would come out and everyone would be watching him then.

He couldn't deal with that, he really couldn't.

"Hey, Carter, you listening to me?"

"I was trying hard not to." Shane drawled out, dodging the pen Andi flung at him.

"Fucker," Andi ground out with a laugh. "I was asking you if you had any issues with me asking Shannon to come back and do the photoshoot with our A-listers? I know she had a massive hard-on for you, but her stuff is good, really good. I just need to sign off on it and then have the unenviable task of trying to get the band, the racers, Oli, Danika, and hopefully JJ all in the one room."

Shane shrugged, telling Andi he didn't care, but he was a little freaked out about it all. It had been bound to happen sooner rather than later, but Shane hadn't been prepared for it. It had taken a few days for his appetite to come back, and he'd been working out more than he was supposed to.

He wanted to retreat to Manchester. He wanted to book a flight right out of this country that brought out the parts of him that he despised. He fucking hated feeling like this. However, Shane had made a promise to Eve, and he didn't go back on his word.

"I spoke to Noah the other night about getting NQL racing on board. He said he'd talk it over with the lads and see how they felt. It would be good promo for Luke and Jack, while they were waiting to get cleared and ready to rally."

Andi's eyes widened. "Shit, good call. I didn't even think about them. Jack is a little showy fucker anyways and Luke did a few shoots when he was in F1. We need to get him, Jack, a PA. Any of those CV's take your fancy?"

"There was one, and when I talked to her on the phone, she had all the relevant experience. I liked her. I'm just not sure if it will cause friction, with who her brother is."

Andi's gaze narrowed as Shane routed out the CV and handed it to her. He watched her eyes scan the pages, then her brows shot up. "Damn, no way."

"Yup. I mean who her brother is doesn't matter. She has all the right qualifications for the role and was even willing to do some courses to upskill. If I had to pick someone to join my team, then I'd want her."

Andi smirked, wiggling her eyebrows. "Your team, is it?"

Shane realized his mistake the moment he'd said it and couldn't walk it back now. "Well, you and Charlie promised me a promotion and since you know jack shit about anything sports related, I'd want an equal shot at head of the sports department. I can't manage everyone, so I'd need some minions."

"You think you're that good, Carter?" Andi retorted, clearly amused.

"I know I am, Collins. Or you wouldn't have harassed me for months to come over here and do what I do. Don't play coy now you think you've won. I could be an asshole and tell you that I've had inquiries from other PR consultancies now that Rebel PR is pulling out of the UK."

Andi's gaze narrowed. "Who you been talking to?"

Shane shrugged and gave Andi a smug smile. "I haven't been talking to anyone. They've been emailing me and blowing up my phone."

"Spill it, Carter. Don't be a prick."

Shane sighed, then listed out the firms that had been in contact with him, name-dropping some big names and then he threw in another name that had Andi scoffing.

"Well, I know there is no way you would go and work for Garrett so don't even bother name-dropping him. Dude only runs his company cause Daddy bought it for him. you'd have to be insane to work for him."

"The money he's offering is insane."

"Money isn't everything, Carter. What about job satisfaction?"

"I think I'd be pretty satisfied driving the hundred-grand company car round Manchester." Shane was only trying to rile her up, and it was working because Andi was glaring at him like he's just admitted that he liked to kick puppies or some shit.

"So, that's all it takes to get you into bed? A company car and a sleaze who's had more HR complaints and court dates for sexual harassment. Are you that cheap?"

Fuck, he'd not expected her to be hissing back at him like that. Shane thought Andi knew him better than to think he'd be that desperate for a job that he'd take a job from a man who skirted a line between being creepy and being a rapist.

"Christ Collins, I was only messing. I told Garret to fuck off and that there was no offer out there that would make me come work for him, especially since I was actively trying to steal some of his clients out from under him. Hell, half his sports roster called me and asked if they could jump ship. And you would think you'd know me better than to think I'd go there with him of all people."

Andi blew out a breath. "Fuck, shit. I'm sorry. I *know* that. I'm just tired and hangry and look, I don't like admitting weakness but if you back off now, if you walk, I don't think I can do it all when Charlie goes on maternity leave. I'm spreading myself too thin as it is and now Declan's pissed at me because I suggested postponing the wedding plans."

Jesus, it must be bad if Andi was telling him all about this. Andi was one of the most private people he knew and why the hell had she wanted to postpone her wedding? She'd already waited ages to set a date because of the workload.

"It's grand, Andi. And we just need more staff. You keep bringing in work and we don't have enough people for it all. I'll tell Karla to come over for a face-to-face, that's a start. I'll look at the other CVs and see who looks good. I'll filter out the no's, and then we can choose who to invite to interview."

Andi sagged in her chair. "You sticking around then? For good?"

Shane snorted, leaning back in his chair. "For now. I won't make any promises, Andi. I told you before that coming back to Cork brings up a lot of shit I don't want to deal with. It's not gonna be as easy for me as it was for you, or Charlie. Hell, even Ronan. I'm here to help for now, and that will have to be enough today, okay? I will do what's best for me in the end."

And that's why you've been alternating from starving yourself to bingeing and purging? You're doing what's best for you? How's that working out for you?

Shane flinched at the sound of his dad's voice in his head, and it must have shown on his face, because Andi's face softened. He got to his feet, citing having to check in with Eve at the gym. Shutting down his computer, Shane was almost to the door when Andi called his name.

"Don't tell Charlie about my outburst. She doesn't need to worry about me. And thanks, for staying to help me. I do appreciate it even if I don't always say it."

Shane leaned against the doorframe for a second. "It's grand. I won't tell Charlie. Just make sure you don't go full Andrea Collins and try and do it all yourself. There'll be no Rebel PR if you end up sick or run yourself into the ground. There is no I in Team, Collins."

He walked out the door to Andi's laughter and the tension in his chest eased just a tad.

CHAPTER FOURTEEN

Eve

EVE FOUND that the one thing she missed about being in Liverpool apart from being able to find a Greggs on nearly every damn corner, was the lack of available sparring partners. With Noah and Quinn gearing up to leave for the new Formula 1 season, and even Andi's Declan heading off for some music promo, until the gym had a few more clients, Eve was stuck without a sparring partner.

She'd tried to persuade Darren to come and go a few rounds with her, but he'd told her that his face was too pretty for her to damage. Eve had rolled her eyes, then cheekily asked Cathal if he wanted to come and get sweaty with her. He had just rolled his eyes, cheeks a little redder, and ignored Eve's attempts to flirt with him.

She'd never go there knowing Cathal and Luna were solid, but they had been doing this back-and-forth teasing since Eve was a teenager, and Cathal knew it was harmless. Hell, even Luna got a kick out of it according to Darren.

And like hell if she was gonna ask Abercrombie to rock up and help a girl out.

Eve had gone full stalker the moment she had gotten back to her photoshoot. She had enough restraint until after she had showered and gotten into comfy clothes before dragging out her laptop and googling Shane Carter. Hours had passed by as Eve just watched the athleticism of the man who kept the sheer strength he possessed tightly under wraps.

God, Shane was magnificent. Eve didn't know much about gymnastics but damn, she knew about strength and grace and just raw talent, and Shane Carter had that in buckets. The cocky arrogance that Eve had put down to him being a guy was now totally understandable.

Annoying, but totally understandable.

It didn't help either that since getting a look at the toned physical underneath all the clothes, Eve kept wondering if he still looked that good now.

As if she had conjured him into being, the man himself strode through the doors of the gym. He was wearing grey sweatpants hung how on his hips, a black tee that was just a little snug, and Eve was here for it. Eve thought he would look better without his clothes.

Eve did her best to ignore him, going about her routine with the freestanding punch bag. She could feel the weight of his eyes on her, and Eve kept her eyes on the punching bag, and off of Shane Carter.

After like, ten minutes, Eve got prickly about him standing there, with his arms crossed over his chest and she grabbed the bag and glared at him. "You gonna stand there all day watching me?"

"Well, since it seems to be annoying you so much, I might just do that."

Eve snorted at his teasing tone. "Don't you know it's not

wise to tease a woman who could and has given you a bloody nose?"

"I wasn't ready for you the last time. I'm ready now."

I'm ready now.

Fuck if that tone didn't make her want to lick him right up.

Eve shook her head and went back to punching the bag. She hit it once, twice, then harder the next one so it shook out of reach until Shane stepped forward and grabbed the sides of it, steadying it. Eve blew her hair out of her face, then reached down to take up her water bottle.

"You're frustrated."

Fuck was she that easy to read?

Eve arched a brow, as if daring Shane to call her out on it. His lips quirked, like he was trying not to smile, and she wanted to either kiss or punch that look off his face. He didn't elaborate on his comment, just let go of the bag and exhaled through his nose.

"I put in a few calls to try and see if any of our potential clients were up to sparring with you. Luke's done some with Noah and Quinn, so he should be a good partner. Jack's a little bit of a wild card and probably not the best fit."

Eve chuckled. "You think I couldn't handle him?"

"More like he couldn't handle you," Shane said, his curving into a slow, sexy smile. "I would fucking hate to get a phone call from Noah at stupid o'clock in the morning after you broke pretty boy's face or worse, his arm or leg. He can still drive a car with a busted face, can't rally if you break a limb."

"You have that much faith in my ability to fight?"

"Yes."

No waver, no hesitation. Just pure certainly in his tone and that made her inside flip flop.

Shane walked around and Eve watched as he walked in a

straight line. She recognised what he was doing from one of his online videos. Men didn't compete in the beam, but Shane had done it with ease. He'd excelled at it as if he was as light as the female gymnasts that competed.

"Luke and Jack are off looking at some special equipment Jack needs for his car, but Luke will come by when he gets a chance. In the meantime, looks like you're stuck with me."

That gave Eve pause.

"No. Not happening."

Shane lifted both his brows. "Afraid you couldn't handle me?"

Oh yeah, she could handle him. Eve could handle him any way that he wanted and then some.

"I'd hate to break your nose for real this time."

Shane walked the line back toward his original starting point. "I goaded you last time to hit me. I deserved that. I used to spar at least once a week in Manchester with one of the lads, and while I might not be UFC standard, I get by."

Eve was about to protest, but Shane just jumped up on the side of the ring and gracefully got into the boxing ring. He started to stretch, and Eve just stood there watching him. Shane's process was different to hers, like he was used to making sure his limbs were as flexible as possible. She supposed being a gymnast meant that he was very, very flexible, and that had her mind drifting to ridiculously dirty thoughts about angles and positions.

"Come on, Barbie, let's go party."

Eve glared at him and that made him laugh. "You did not just call me fucking Barbie."

Shane held his hands up. "Hey, I had to get you pissed enough to agree to spar with me. I saw the video of what you did to the young fella who called you that. At least I haven't yanked on your ponytail."

That sent a shot of heat right in between her legs.

Eve slid into the ring, then got to her feet and bounced. "All right, Abercrombie, last chance to back out."

Shane cracked his neck and then grinned before going full Neo and beckoning her forward with his hand. Eve waited half a heartbeat before she advanced. She was quick on her feet, but so was Shane. They danced around one another, sizing each other up.

Eve toyed with him a little, and they traded a few love taps back and forth. He was very good and was keeping her close within striking range. She punched hard but she kicked even harder. Shane must have checked out some of her videos and studied how she liked to move, and how she liked to strike. Once Eve had them bruised from her kicks, she moved in, getting real close until she could get an armbar locked in or even a chokehold.

Shane telegraphed a move, and Eve blocked it, then struck out with her foot and kicked him in the side. Abercrombie let out a grunt that had Eve grinning and Shane rubbed at his side for a second until he lifted eyes filled with amusement and a little something else that had adrenaline running through her veins.

Shane laughed, shaking his head. "Don't look so cocky, Barbie. That was a lucky shot."

Eve grinned back at him, then gave him a mock little bow. "Not lucky. Just talented."

Shane lunged and Eve managed to dodge his jab, kicking out again and catching him again in the side. This time, she didn't relent. Eve did one of her one-two punch combos, making Shane retreat into the centre of the ring and right where Eve wanted him.

"You'll never beat me from all the way over there."

Eve could see the blaze of heat in his eyes as he advanced toward her. Eve put up her hands and Shane focused on her fists when he should have been watching her legs. Lightning quick, Eve swept out her leg, catching Shane. He went down with a grunt to the mat, and Eve pumped her fist in the air.

"Ha! Take that, Abercrombie."

Shane stared up at her and Eve stepped over him, always gracious in her victory as she stuck her tongue out at him. Shane watched her for a split second, then she felt his hands on her ankles between one breath and the next and then she was straddling his rock-hard abs and her hands were on his chest to steady herself. Their eyes clashed, and Eve couldn't stop herself from grabbing the front of Shane's T-shirt, and hauling him up for a kiss.

CHAPTER FIFTEEN

Shane

THE MOMENT EVE'S lips crashed into his, Shane was rock hard. Hell, he had been struggling not to get amped up during their back-and-forth banter. Eve kissed the way she fought, hard, hot, and sinfully dirty. Her teeth sank into his bottom lip, forcing him to open up and the sweep of her tongue had him burning up.

Shane sat up further, causing Eve to slide down so that she hooked her legs around his waist. Eve arched her hips to his and she moaned into his mouth. His hands slipped down to cup her ass, holding her exactly where he wanted her without the barrier of clothes. Eve moved her hands from the front of his tee, slipping up to slide into his hair. Shane's heart was racing as she scraped her nails along his scalp.

Eve rocked her hips against his and when she broke the kiss to take in a gulp of air, Shane had a moment of clarity to remember that they were essentially making out in the middle of the gym where anyone could walk in, and there were cameras everywhere.

Their eyes clashed and Eve dipped her head as if to kiss him again and if she did, Shane knew he wouldn't care about who the hell could walk in and catch them if she kept looking at him like she was.

"Eve," Shane started, his hand shifting up to grip her hips to stop Eve from rocking against his hard-on. "Wait, just wait a second."

Eve paused and cupped the sides of his neck. "Please don't tell me that you are really gonna be Mr. Sensible and tell me we can't do this because of client whatsit or whatever."

Shane shook his head, tightening his grip on her hips. "No, I wasn't even thinking that. But there are cameras and an open fucking door and once I get you naked, I don't want to be interrupted."

Eve gave him this sinful grin as she kissed him hard on the lips and then the heat of her body was gone off him and Shane laid back down and groaned. He rolled up into a standing position, and followed Eve out of ring, grabbing their things before heading out and across the road.

They stood on opposite sides of the elevator, eyes on one another. Eve pulled her crop top over her head, strutting out the moment the doors pinged open. There were no words said between them as Eve went to her apartment, opened the door, and went inside.

Shane knew he should walk away. But the way Eve looked at him, untainted by the shameful things he kept secret, Shane felt like he was himself in that moment. And if he could steal just one sliver of normality, was that the worst thing in the world?

He followed Eve into her apartment to find her waiting for him. She crooked a finger at him, and he arched a brow. Eve chuckled, this low, husky sound that had him striding forward and capturing her lips with his. They moved, as if they were dancing a routine until Eve's back hit the wall and Shane pressed into her. Shane broke the kiss and kissed down the column of her throat, a groan escaping her lips and it gave Shane's confidence a massive boost.

Slipping a hand between their bodies, Shane dipped his fingers inside her tiny scrap of kickers, and let out a moan of his own. "Fuck, you're drenched."

Eve opened her mouth to respond but Shane slid a finger inside her, and whatever she was about to say was covered with a moan of her own. She writhed against his hand, encouraging him, and then he added a second finger when he thrust inside her and he felt her clench around him,

Damn, he couldn't wait to feel her do that to his cock.

But first, he needed a taste of her.

Dropping to his knees, Shane placed a hand on Eve's taunt stomach to hold her in place as he dragged down her knickers, giving her enough space to kick them off. He leaned in and pressed a kiss to her thigh, felt her shiver, then lifted one leg over his shoulder and licked a languid line along her core. Her legs trembled, and Shane looked up at her for a moment before he got back to the task at hand.

He licked and sucked and alternated between thrusting two fingers inside her and using his tongue. The noises Eve was making were like music to his ears, and when she moaned his name, long and sultry, his cock pulsed, wanting out and inside this woman who made him feel invincible.

He could tell that Eve was close, she writhed against his face, urging him to go faster, and when Shane grazed his teeth against her most sensitive flesh, his name sounded like a curse as Eve came hard. He licked and petted her through her release.

"Dammit, Abercrombie," she gasped as Shane slide her leg off his shoulder, his hands on her hips to keep her upright. "Please tell me you are as good with your cock as you are with your tongue."

Shane gave her a lopsided grin, and then kissed her again.

He was five seconds away from mounting her right there against the wall at the way Eve was eagerly grinding against him, when he dragged his lips from hers and trailed them down to the swell of her breasts. He pressed an open-mouthed kiss to her breast and then she was shoving down his joggers and putting her hand on his cock.

"Fuck." He ground out, his hips jerking forward, eager to have Eve's hands fisting his cock. He had a moment to process, and he pulled back to swear. "Condoms?"

Eve arched a brow. "As in multiple? I'm on board with that."

Shane chuckled and rested his forehead against hers. "No, smartass. I meant do you have condoms because I have none on me and I want in you so fucking bad."

Eve took his hand and led him down to her bedroom. They kissed a little on the way, slower, more deliberate, and when Eve stripped off her bra and stood gloriously naked in front of him, ruffling in her drawer and taking out a box and opening them to put a few on the locker.

Shane pressed his front against her back, and wound a hand into her ponytail. He gave her hair a gentle but firm tug, and she looked over her shoulder at him. Her cheeks were flushed, and there was this intense heat in Eve's eyes that made them look brighter, and sharper.

Eve turned in his arms and he let go of her ponytail to divest himself of his clothes. He was suddenly self-conscious of the tattoo on his chest and he waited for Eve to ask him about it. She traced her fingers over the outline of it, and then she was ripping open the foil wrapper.

She rolled the condom on, stroking his cock before and after it was on, then they were kissing again. He was too amped up to go slow and it seemed like Eve was right on board with that.

"Fuck me, Abercrombie. Don't hold back. I want to feel you in me all day tomorrow."

Shane hooked an arm around her waist and hoisted Eve up. She balanced on his hips as he backed her against the wall. Moving in sync, they aligned their bodies and then Shane was sliding into her. He tried to take his time, pushing in slowly as Eve's body clenched and shifted to accommodate him. That was until she thrust downward as he slid in and then he was seated fully inside her.

They stilled for just a second like it was a crack before the lightning. Shane wasn't sure who moved first, but then he was pounding into her, her breasts bouncing with each thrust. Eve locked her arms around his neck, as Shane fucked her against the wall and then she was coming around his cock and he tried hard not to find his own release just yet.

Moving forward, still buried deep inside her, Shane threw her down on the bed, keeping up his furious pace until Eve scored her nails down his back and she told him that she was coming again. Her walls clenched tighter this time with her orgasm, and that dragged Shane over the edge as he moaned her name and his balls tightened and then he was coming right along with her.

When they both recovered from the intensity of what just happened, Shane reluctantly pulled out of her, disposing of the condom as Eve went to the bathroom. He lay down on the bed, and Eve crawled in beside him. Shane wrapped an arm around her and pulled her closer, as Eve grabbed her fingers along his sternum. She pressed her lips to his chest, and his cock twitched, causing Eve to look at him with an amused expression.

"Again?"

Shane grinned, rolling so that he pinned Eve under him, and kissed and touched and stroked Eve until he convinced her to go another round.

CHAPTER SIXTEEN

Eve

EVE WOKE up the following morning because she was too hot. That wasn't surprising considering she had Shane laying half on her, half off, his thick muscular leg thrown over her. Shane also had an arm across her body, just below her breasts. His eyes were closed, his breathing even as Eve felt the press of his cock against her stomach, and even though they had had a lot of sex last night, she was wondering if they had enough energy for another round.

Who needed cardio when Shane Carter fucked her like he had last night?

Every muscle in her body ached in the best possible way. Eve felt all the warm endorphins that she got after a fight, the ones that made her feel euphoric, even if her body was battered. She'd marvelled at the way Shane hadn't held back with her last night, hadn't treated her like she was breakable, and had taken her roughly just like she wanted to be taken.

Oh, he'd tried to be gentle with her when he thought he was being too rough, had waited for Eve to consent before they had crashed together and damn, she wanted to do it all over again.

Eve traced her fingers along the length of the arm across her chest. Shane's leg slid down a little as he moved in his sleep, that muscular thigh sliding right between her legs, pressing against her sensitive clit and she moaned, rubbing herself against it.

She turned her head and watched as Shane's eyes started to open and for a moment, he looked at her with this hazy expression, unguarded, and her stomach did a somersault. His hand slipped up to cup her breast, squeezing hard enough that it blurred the line between pleasure and pain. Eve arched up into his touch, felt the hardness of his erection and Eve just had to have him inside her again.

Shane shifted like he was going to roll on top of her, but Eve used the momentum to reverse their positions so that she straddled his waist. Leaning down, she kissed him hard once on the lips then scampered off the bed.

"Hold that thought."

Shane's chuckle made her core clench, as Eve went to the bathroom and then walked back out to see Shane stroking his cock. Jesus, her mouth watered. She grabbed a condom from the bedside table and then went to the end of the bed and crawled up until she put the condom down to place her hands on Shane's thighs.

His eyes burned with heat as she watched him stroke once more, then Eve wrapped her hand around the base of his shaft. "Let me."

Her voice came out husky, and when Shane released his hold on his cock, Eve ran her hand up and down the hot hard flesh before she lowered her mouth and licked up the length of it. It was hot and salty and all Shane as he moaned and fisted his hands in the sheets. Lowering her mouth, Eve took him into her mouth, and it took her a few minutes to accommodate his size.

She moved up and down, taking more of him into her mouth until she had taken all she could. She gagged, then took a few breaths in through her nose before Eve started to suck and lick and taste. Shane let out a long curse as his fingers slid into her hair, tugging, and telling her what he needed from her.

Eve couldn't stand the ache between her legs and she had to slip her fingers along her core, as she moaned around Shane's shaft, and he jerked in her mouth. When she grazed her teeth along the molten skin, he growled and yanked her hair hard and she pulled her mouth off his cock with a pop.

She had faced down opponents in the ring, across a stage during weigh-ins, people who underestimated her, but the way Shane held her gaze right there and then, lust, and heat, and all fucking sexiness, Eve had a feeling that she could fall for this man.

"Condom." He ground out, like he was trying to hold himself back.

Eve reached for the condom, opened the packet, and then rolled it before she angled the tip at her entrance. She normally needed a little more foreplay to get her ready for sex, and yet, Shane just had to look at her and she was wet for him, as if she'd already had an orgasm. Eve started to lower herself down, inch by blistering inch as Shane's hands snapped out and gripped her hips.

He pulled her down as his hips thrust upward, until he was sheathed inside her. Eve threw her head back and groaned, her palms slapping his bare chest. Eve started to move, but like hell if she was sure if she was the one that was the one that was moving or if Shane was using his strength to make her ride him.

Who the fuck cared when it felt so good?

The familiar quiver in her core told her she was close to orgasm, and she started to rise up and slide back down a little harder, searching for the pure ecstasy of oblivion. Shane's grip tightened on her hips, holding her in place, and Eve let out a whimper in protest, earning her a dark chuckle from the infuriating man driving her insane.

"Oh god, Shane, I'm close. Come on, just fuck me with that glorious cock of yours."

Said cock twitched inside her, as Shane snaked a hand around her waist and pushed himself off the bed so that their faces were inches from one another. He did it with such little effort, like it was a natural movement for him, and Eve trembled around him.

His other hand came up to brush his thumb along her lower lip. Their eyes clashed, the intimacy of looking into each other's eyes while he was buried deep inside her shattered her. Eve came apart in his arms as Shane's kiss muffled her cries. He plunged his tongue into her mouth and then he started to move them both, so the moment she came down from riding one wave, she was already cresting a second.

The arch of his hips became more hurried, more insistent, and when he hit her a little deeper after angling their bodies, Eve came hard again, like she'd gotten sucker punched and her entire body just shaking. She felt Shane's body tense as she clung to him and then he was saying her name as he thrust into her once more and found his own release.

They stayed locked in place for a couple of minutes, both of them breathing hard, sweat on their bodies and Eve wasn't sure she could feel her legs. Shane buried his face in the curve of her neck, his breath hot against her flesh and she shivered.

"Are you cold?" Came his strained voice.

"Fuck no," Eve said with a laugh. "I feel like I've been on a 5k run. I don't think my legs work."

Shane chuckled, then slid them both down to the edge of

the bed. she marvelled at the way he got up off the bed, and pulled out of her in a slow way that made her swear and clench around him, like her fucking pussy was trying to hold him where it liked him. Once her feet were on the ground, Shane kissed her slowly, and then she went to go pee, and he got rid of the condom.

Unfortunately, when she came out of the bathroom, Shane had pulled on his boxers, but was sitting on the bed. His eyes scanned over her body, and he smiled. Damnit if she wouldn't love to know what was going on in his head.

Her stomach rumbled, making her laugh. "Right, as much as I would love to drag you back into that bed and see how flexible you could get, I'm fucking starving. I feel like last night and this morning burned away any carbs I ate in the last couple of days so how about we shower, and then you and me can go somewhere and get breakfast? I swear I could murder a full Irish."

The heat vanished from Shane's eyes. The switch was instantaneous and gone was the smiling teasing man who had talked dirty to her last night. Hell, it was like someone had poured cold water over him he was up and pulling on his sweatpants so fast, Eve was surprised Shane didn't fall over.

"I ...ugh, no. Look this was fun and all, but I gotta go. I got carried away and it shouldn't have happened. It can't happen again. No. It really can't."

Eve opened her mouth to answer, but didn't get the chance. Shane grabbed his t-shirt and shoes and bolted out of her room like the guards were chasing him. Eve heard the front door slam shut so hard it made her jump and she sat down on the edge of the bed.

What the fuck had just happened?

Chapter Seventeen

Shane

SHANE CLOSED the front door of his apartment with an audible bang, dropped his clothes on the floor, and leaned against the door, trying to calm the rapid racing of his heart. Closing his eyes, he banged his head against the door, the sharp pain in the back of his head clearing some of his panic.

Fuck...fuck.... *fuck.*

For a blissful moment, Shane had forgotten that he was defective. He'd been so absorbed in her, in Eve, in making her come that he hadn't given a second thought to the things that kept him shackled to the past. He'd just been a man in the arms of a beautiful woman who was strong, but she had trembled at his touch.

And it had been amazing. It had been fanfuckingtastic and Shane had to go and fuck it all up the moment Eve had mentioned about going for food. As soon as she had told him she was starving, instead of taking it as the compliment it was meant to be, Shane's heart had started to beat so hard he thought it might come out of his chest. Panic flared in his chest and if he had to sit down to breakfast with Eve, she'd have seen past his façade and realized that he was weak and pathetic and broken inside.

Pushing off the door, Shane left his clothes where he'd thrown them, because he could smell Eve on them, hell, he could smell her on his skin, and his brain was telling him to make himself sick and then go back over and apologize and kiss her until she forgets that he had thrown a strop.

Stripping off the remainder of his clothes, Shane turned on the shower and stepped inside. The water hit him at full force, and he jerked back, remembering the time he had been late to training one morning because he'd stayed over at Ronan's for his birthday, and they'd slept in.

His dad had been waiting at the new gym that he'd installed after the events at the training centre, so Shane could work out at home. Shane could tell from the look in his eyes that his dad was pissed that he was late, especially with the competition Shane had in a couple of weeks in Paris.

Henry had ordered him to get changed into his workout gear, and the moment Shane stepped into the gym and his dad closed the door, Shane had never wanted to run away more in his life.

"I told you not to be late, lad."

"I'm sorry, Dad. Ronan's mam had a work emergency and could only drop me home now. I did text you." Shane said, *stretching his limbs because he knew his dad would work him to death today as punishment for being late.*

"You will be sorry. I promise ya. Now, what fucking junk food did that boy make you eat while you were sleeping over?"

His dad didn't like Ronan, and said he was a bad influence on Shane. But his dad didn't like Ronan's parents either because they were letting him be an actor and encouraging a career that his dad felt was stupid, and unrewarding.

"I uh, we uh."

His dad grabbed the collar of his t-shirt. "Don't stutter. You might be simple, but you aren't that fucking stupid. Tell me."

Shane lied his ass off, giving his dad a little of what he had eaten and not the full extent. His dad might forgive him a few slices of pizza and a bottle of Coke, but if he told his dad about the cake and the sweets, and the ice cream that Shane had devoured, there would be war.

Taking out his phone, his dad did some calculations, and then Shane could almost see the gleeful smile curving his lips that Shane was in for a world of hurt.

"In order to be at optimal weight, you need to burn off all the junk food you shoved into your mouth last night. run it off. Now, Shane. Run it fucking off."

Shane ran. He had little choice but to run until his dad told him to stop. Henry didn't tell him to stop though, and left Shane to run and run around the four corners of the gym, until his lungs burned, his legs felt like jelly, and all the food he had eaten last night was simmering inside his stomach ready for him to spew.

He managed to open the door and step into the yard before he upchucked all over the concrete. His stomach hurt so bad and he didn't think that his legs would hold him up. Shane didn't know how long he was sick, but after he felt dizzy and wrecked. He wanted to crawl into bed and sleep.

But his dad had other ideas.

Shane's heart had been pounding inside his chest so loud that Shane hadn't heard anything. He didn't hear his dad coming out to the yard. Didn't hear him coming toward Shane and he didn't hear him at the garden hose until the frigid cold water hit him at full force.

Shane staggered back, spluttering, begging his dad to stop, but Henry just laughed, telling Shane it was the least he deserved for trying to ruin all the hard work that he had put in to make Shane the best. It was not Henry's fault that his son was weak and pathetic and didn't realize the golden ticket. Henry had to prove that he had been right all along, and his stupid bitch of a mother had been wrong.

The deluge of water eventually stopped, and Shane stood, drenched, shivering in the winter coldness. His teeth chattered and water dripped down from his hair. His dad glared at him until Shane turned around and made to go back into the house to change.

"And where the fuck do you think you are going?"

"Dad, I'm soaking. I need to get changed so I don't get sick."

Henry scoffed. "Maybe you'll learn a lesson then. Get your ass in that gym and I want a hundred pull-ups on the bar. No half-assing it, lad or you'll start over and over until I'm satisfied. Move!"

Shane had done what his father had wanted, he's done a hundred pull-ups, drenched to the bone, shivering from the cold, under his dad's watchful eye. But at least with the water still dripping from his hair, Shane was able to mask the tears that slipped free and trickled down his cheeks.

Thankfully, his dad hadn't seen him cry...it would have been way worse if that happened.

When Shane emerged from the memory, he was sat on the floor of the shower, his head in his hands and he was shaking. His heart was racing, and he had this gnawing hunger in his stomach. He didn't remember the last time he'd eaten a full meal, and he tried not to think about the fact that being back in this city, in this country, had made it so easy for him to fall back into bad habits.

He hated not feeling like he was in control. Fucking *despised* it.

Shane was moving before he put any conscious thought into it, dressing hurriedly even though he was still wet. Once he had pants and a t-shirt on, he went out to the kitchen and paced. He paced the entire length of his apartment like a caged animal. Shane gripped the strands of his hair, wanting to scream out his frustration.

He could go back to Manchester. He could say fuck it and tell Andi that he couldn't do it. Shane was faltering here, alone, ruining any hopes that moving back to Cork would be a viable option for him. This city would kill him. It had been killing him since the day his dad had realized that he was good at gymnastics, and he'd seen gold medals in Shane's future.

Shane glanced at his phone. He could ring Ronan. He could call Andi. He could walk over to the woman across the hall and tell her what was happening to him. He could get all the secrets off his chest and just breathe. Shane could take an easy breath for the first time in his life.

Then they'll all know that you are weak...

Shame was an evil demon, instilled in him by his dad all those years ago. Shane knew what he should do, and yet, he couldn't do it. He couldn't ask for help...

Storming over to the kitchen drawer he yanked it out, taking the entire drawer with him as he dumped the contents onto the coffee table. Shane sank down to the ground and grabbed a large bar of chocolate. Ripping the package open, he all but shoved the bar into his mouth. The sugar rush and the taste made him groan, and Shane told himself it was just this one and then he would stop. He would stop.

After the next one.

After this one.

When it was all gone, and he didn't feel empty inside.

CHAPTER EIGHTEEN

Shane

SHANE FELT LIKE SHIT.

The comedown after the overload of food had been swift. He'd demolished his stash and sat in the carnage of it all before he'd bolted to the bathroom to stick his fingers back his throat to purge it all from his system. It was so bad that he'd spent at least a half an hour after he'd made himself sick empty retching and spewing up bile. Shane had ignored his phone, ignored the knock on his door, and had fallen asleep curled in a ball on the bathroom floor.

He'd slept for a solid twelve hours, not even waking at his normal time of just gone half four. Instead, his watch told him that it was a little after six. He went through the motions of showering, dressing, drinking one of his protein shakes, and forcing himself to eat a nutrition bar because he felt dizzy. His throat burned and his stomach felt like he'd taken a punch to it.

When he stepped back into the living room, Shane's heart sank at the chocolate wrappers, the empty crisp packages, and the empty sweet bags. He made himself clean away the evidence of his relapse, then grabbed his keys, his phone, his earbuds, and slipped his feet into his trainers.

He just needed to get out of this cage and clear his head.

Shane had already decided that he couldn't stay in Cork. He had made the mistake of agreeing to come back here, and if it meant that he had to quit the job he loved to be free of this place then he had to do it.

Running away again? Typical fucking Shane, running when things are tough...just like your mother.

Shane flinched, remembering his dad's parting words to him when Shane had told him that he was done with gymnastics. Henry had never expected Shane to really walk away, but Shane knew that if he was to be free of his dad, then he had to leave behind the sport he loved.

He let himself be lost in the music, no real destination in mind but Shane wasn't surprised when his feet brought him to the last place that he'd felt truly happy. Little Leaps Gymnastics looked the exact same as it had when Shane had come here as a child. He'd loved it all, the teachers, the other students who were his friends and not the competition, the joy of landing a move and everyone cheering for him.

Then his dad had taken him out of here when he was a teen to focus on a more grueling regime and the joy of the sport had started to fade. He started to resent it. He started to hate the fact that he was good at it, that the sport had turned his father into a monster and pushed his mother out the door.

He wanted to go inside. He wanted to see if the joy that he was missing had somehow been abandoned in that building, waiting for him to come and collect it again. Shutting off the music, part of Shane was afraid that he'd walk in there and find no joy, and the finality that he would never find it again would truly be the death of him. At least he could pretend standing outside that the little boy he once was still in there, tumbling and doing cartwheels and back flips to his heart's content.

"May I help you?"

Shane hadn't heard the car drive up, or noticed the woman walking toward him he was so lost in his thoughts. He opened his mouth to tell her he was grand and just leaving, when he recognised the person standing in front of him.

"I was just reminiscing. I don't know if you remember me, Mrs. Ryan, I used to go here."

The woman narrowed her gaze, studied him, and then her mouth formed an O. "My goodness, Shane Carter. It is good to see you."

Shane gave his former teacher a small smile. "And you. It looks the same from out here. I think the happiest years of my life happened in that building."

Maybe it was the way he said it, or how shite he looked but Mrs. Ryan reached out and put a hand on his arm. "Would you like to come in? There should be no one due to come in until ten this morning so it will be just you and me. We could have a cup of tea and a chat."

Shane looked away. "I really shouldn't."

"Nonsense," she replied with a smile. "You can keep this old woman company and have the space to have a look around. Come now, let's get in out of the cold."

Shane trailed after her, feeling apprehensive about it all, but the moment he ducked inside and stood just off all the mats, Shane closed his eyes and inhaled. It smelled the same as he remembered. It felt the same as he remembered, and his throat felt thick with emotion. The silence was comforting, and Shane realized that he *had* missed this, the sense of anticipation, the sense of freedom and peace that he had found in gymnastics that his dad had robbed him of.

Kicking off his shoes, Shane took a tentative step onto the mats, a giddiness spreading through his chest. He walked around, trailing his fingers along the apparatus, an overwhelming urge to just throw caution to the wind and see if he could still do it, if he could still be a gymnast at least for fun.

When was the last time he'd done anything for fun?

He couldn't bear to look at the rings and not flinch, so he walked over to the beam, an apparatus that he didn't compete on, but loved to watch the woman do and had been good at it himself. He set his hands on the beam, a feeling in his chest that he hadn't felt in the longest time, and hoisted himself up so that he straddled it.

It felt strange and familiar all at once, and with his hands braced on the beam, Shane pushed himself up to try and go into a handstand. His hands slipped off the beam and he landed in a heap on the mat. He waited for his dad's voice to bounce round in his head, and when he heard nothing, Shane just laughed and got back up.

This time, when he went into a handstand, he held it, then lowered his feet to steady himself on the beam. He braced his feet, then walked the length of it, up and down, until he felt comfortable that he could hold his balance. He did a spin, came out of it a little shaky, and he laughed, the sound filling the empty gym.

Shane closed his eyes, feeling the beam under his feet as he moved, then he came to the end of the beam and said, fuck it, let's see if he still had it. Turning so that he was facing the other way, Shane did a double handstand and tried to do a tumble into dismount. If he had pulled it off, it would have looked fucking epic, however, he landed on his ass after overrotating.

The urge to get back up and accept the challenge that he could hit it rushed through his veins and Shane grinned, chuckling softly to himself. The joy he'd been searching for was still here and he wanted to do it all again.

Fuck he'd missed it.

"You've still got it."

Shane peered up to see Mrs. Ryan smiling down at him, two cups of tea in her hand. Leaping to his feet, Shane took the mug she held out to him, and he took a sip. "I hadn't realized how much I missed it. Is it really strange to say that it feels like I've been missing a limb for eight years and have just found it?"

Mrs. Ryan's smile deepened. "Not strange at all. When something has been a part of your life for so long, when it's taken away, the loss can be immense. Did you allow yourself to grieve it?"

Shane shook his head, unable to verbalize how much what Mrs. Ryan had said made so much sense to him. In one single sentence, she had managed to sum it all up in a way Shane never could have. It settled in him, and something in him healed a little.

"Could I stay a while, please? I need to know if I'm still me."

Mrs. Ryan took the mug from his hand. "You stay as long as you like. And come back whenever you want. You are among friends here who will cast no judgement. But if you don't want to be around too many people, I'm here most mornings currently. The door is always open to you. Have fun."

Shane laughed as she walked away, the woman having no idea just how much that offer might have saved his life today. He started to stretch out his limbs, knowing he would be sore as fuck if he pushed too hard but in that moment Shane didn't care. He pretended that he was five years old again and tumbled his way across the mats.

CHAPTER NINETEEN

Eve

EVE WAS in a foul fucking humour.

She'd been baffled by Shane's reaction after they'd spent the night together and his subsequent ghosting. Like a gobshite, Eve had gone across the hall and knocked on his door a couple times and got no answer until she kicked herself in the ass and told herself that she had never chased a man in her life and she sure as shit wasn't going to chase Shane Carter.

Five days had gone by, and she'd only seen that the man was alive when she went to take a piss at nearly six and happened to look out the window and Shane was striding through the industrial estate with a gear bag slung over his shoulder. He didn't head to the gym across the way, no, he headed down the hill.

Was he going to another gym so he could avoid her?

That was a dick move.

She'd gone back to bed and tossed and turned until she decided to take her frustration out in the gym. She'd sweated out her anger and her hurt, then showered in the gym facilities before she was ready to head to the Rebel PR offices to have a meeting with Andi and Shane. She wasn't looking forward to seeing him after how they left things, but her career was in his hands so she could act professional if he could.

She pushed open the door and strode in, grabbing an apple from the fruit bowl at reception before heading into the office space. Andi was standing with her back to Eve, but she could see the other woman staring at her phone.

There was no sign of Abercrombie.

"Hey, am I early? I can come back if ye not ready to have this meeting."

Andi turned, curving her lips into a smile. "Nah, all good. Shane's been held up at another meeting, so he told me to go ahead and sit down with you."

Oh so ya, they were gonna be grownups about this...sure.

Something must have shown in Eve's expression, because Andi set her phone down on one of the desks and put her hands on her hips. "Is there something I should know?"

Eve took a bite of her apple and mumbled around her mouthful. "Nope. All good."

Andi rolled her eyes and snorted. "Why don't I believe you? Hell, I don't even want to know. Come into my office and we can go through some things."

Having picked up her phone, Andi strode into her office, holding the door open while Eve slipped inside and then she closed it behind her. "The shoot went great, and everyone is thrilled with the final photos we agreed on. They've just signed a deal with a massive chain of stores, and they want to have one of your photos on the walls to promote it."

Eve took another bite of her apple, chewed, swallowed, before asking Andi, "Like how massive a chain?"

"Global. Billboards in Times Square, Shanghai, and London. You're about to be world-famous, girl."

Eve leaned back in her seat. "That only matters to me if it

gets me fights. I feel like I want out of my skin I need to fight so badly."

Andi swept her caramel-coloured hair off her shoulder. "Listen, he worked hard to get the deal done, and I hate that he's not here to tell you himself, but there is an exhibition next week, a new venture bringing MMA fighters from all over Ireland to Cork, and Shane got you a headline slot."

That made Eve sit up a little straighter. She set her half-eaten apple on Andi's desk as the other woman continued to talk. "You are second billed, but top female on the card if I'm saying that right. There will be scouts from lots of different corporations there and Shane hired a videographer to film you coming up to the fight, your prep, the day of the fight, and the fight itself. Make a little documentary-style thing and post it to social media."

Eve must have looked a little shocked, because Andi laughed, a massive grin brightening her face. "He works fast, doesn't he? Listen, I know he's MIA today, but Shane showed me his two-year plan to make you a megastar and he's driven to get you there. This exhibition is only the start. It gets you publicity. The promoters are finalizing whether they will show it on TV or whatever but even if it's not on TV, you are the top-billed female on the card."

Eve was trying to take it all in when Andi asked her if she wanted to know who she was fighting against, and Eve waved Andi off. "Doesn't matter who she is, I'll beat her."

Andi laughed at the cockiness in Eve's words. "God, not you too. I swear all you athletes must have activated some competitive gene the minute you all were born."

Eve snorted. "I know your rep, Andi. You've got that gene too or was that some other ballsy woman who strode up to Oli Scott and told him to shove his offer of a good time and sign her damn contract."

They grinned at each other, and Eve wondered if this was

what it was like to be friends with girls. She'd never had that. In school, girls had been jealous of her, and Eve had always found it easier to hang out with than lads, especially since Darren was there to glare at any fellas who thought she'd be an easy lay.

"You look like something big just ran through your mind," Andi said, startling Eve from her thoughts.

Eve rubbed the back of her neck. "This is weird for me. Women being nice to me. I don't have any female friends, hell, I don't even have that many male friends. When you can level them with one leg swipe, most run away. It's nice to have been around Noah and Quinn the last couple of weeks. I've missed the company."

Andi gave her a warm smile. "Well, one thing you will learn now that you're one of us is that we have a great bunch of friends. We all might be connected by partners or family but what you do for a living doesn't matter when we are together. You can come on our next girl's night. Though it might be tamer than they've been in the past with Charlie pregnant and Niamh having a four-month-old."

"I'd like that and appreciate it. You can get too used to being by yourself."

Andi inclined her head and sighed before looking at her phone. "Carter gets like that. He's a tough nut to crack, is our Shane. But he's a great guy. He's usually dependable as hell. I know he kept who he used to be from you, however, he still trains like a crazy amount. He'd work with you if you asked him."

Eve felt her cheeks heat and Andi gave her an amused look. "Oh, it's like that is it?"

"Nope, there's nothing. I mean, there's...ya...just no."

Andi barked out a laugh and shook her head. "Listen, if you and Shane do go there then I can't exactly tell you off for hooking up. I'm engaged to the lead singer of the band I manage. Charlie is engaged and having a baby with one of her drivers. Quinn fell for the silent brooding Oskar and she's just like Shane, tough to crack. Go for it. Just don't let it affect work and I'll be happy."

Eve opened her mouth, then closed it, then opened it again making Andi just laugh a little harder. Rubbing her temple, Eve picked up her apple and took another bite just for something to do. When she had swallowed, Eve looked at Andi.

"This is all weird. Girlie chats about boys. Do women even do that in real life?"

The grin Andi gave her was mischievous. "Oh, hell ya. When you have a girl's night with Luna Sullivan and Sorcha Healy, who have no goddamn filter, you learn a lot of things. Wait, you'll see. I check and see when our next night is and add you to the group chat."

They chatted for a while, talking about the exhibition next week, a few appearances Andi knew Shane was working on. Eve asked about Andi's wedding plans, not sure if that was something she should be talking to with her sort of boss, but the conversation was easy, far more so than Eve expected. Eve felt so comfortable that when Andi got a text from Charlie telling her to call over for dinner, and Andi invited Eve, she went along and had a good night.

Eve was exhausted when she got home at a very respectable nine that night, saw the light on in Shane's apartment, and paused in the hallway, debating whether to check in with him or not. She had her fist raised, ready to rap her knuckles on the door when she saw the light switch off under the door, and Eve retreated to her own apartment, telling herself she didn't care what was going on with Shane.

But she was a big, fat, liar...

Chapter Twenty

Eve

Eve had been bouncing off the walls all damn day and she was ready to go. The moment her alarm had gone off she was up and over to the gym to get a light workout in. Shane had already been in the gym when she arrived and they shared a polite, cordial greeting, but Eve would worry about that tomorrow, after her fight.

It was the first time they'd been face to face since what had happened, communicating the last few days via email. He looked happier in himself, and she hated that it annoyed her that it was his time away from her that had taken away the heaviness in his shoulders.

Fuck, when did she become the clingy girl who mooned after a guy who obviously was one and done?

Shane had come over to her as she was about to head back to her apartment to shower and her usual meal before a fight and see if she could calm down her nervous anticipation. He waited until she had gathered all her stuff up, then took the bag from her shoulder, making Eve roll her eyes as they walked out of the gym.

"I know you are trying to be chivalrous and shit, but that weighs nothing, and I am a strong independent woman who can carry her own gym bag."

Shane chuckled, then opened the door for her. "I was trying to make up for being an idiot the other morning. Maybe once the fight is over, we could have a talk? I need to explain myself and today's not that day to do that."

They were standing in the middle of the industrial estate, so Eve faced him and was blunt with him. "If you want to tell me the other day was a mistake and we need to be professional, then no point in prolonging it."

Shane rubbed the back of his neck, his expression sheepish. "No, I wasn't gonna say that. I meant I was wondering if you'd let me take you out on a date. Fuck that sounded cheesy, didn't it?"

Eve laughed, slipped her bag off Shane's shoulder, and then went up on her toes to whisper in his ear. "It was cheesy as fuck, but I'm in."

Then she kissed his cheek and strutted off to get ready, leaving Shane standing there in her wake.

Now that that was settled, Eve was able to get in the zone. She went through her usual routine, sorted through her in-ring gear, packed up her bag, and drank some nutrients when Shane texted her to tell her the car was outside.

To keep herself in the zone, she put on her headphones and cranked the music. She got into the back of the car with Shane, and Andi was on the other side. She ignored them both, setting her bag down on the floor and she leaned forward and closed her eyes until she felt a hand on her arm, Shane letting her know that they had arrived.

She followed Andi and Shane out of the car and into the

back of the venue, still in her own world. Once in her changing room, Eve stripped off her hoodie and her tracksuit. She ignored and quite enjoyed Shane's face when she stripped down to just her knickers and then pulled on her shorts and top. It was a matching blue camo set from that designer and they were fab.

Eve wrapped her feet, then was about to do her wrists when the tape was taken out of her hand and then Shane was wrapping her hands and wrist like he'd done it a million times before, and Eve supposed he had.

"Thanks." She said when he was done and then his lips were moving and she realized she couldn't hear him.

He reached up and slipped the headphones off her ears. "You're welcome. You need anything else?"

She bounced on her feet. "You wanna help me warm up? I promise not to punch you in the nose."

Shane chuckled, taking a step back. "Ya, I'd appreciate you keep those fists of rage for your opponent."

Slipping on some pads, Shane held up his hands and Eve did a few combinations, then threw a kick and then another, before a knock to the door sounded and Andi stuck her head in.

"I just need a word with Shane."

Shane took off the pads and slipped out the door, closing it behind him. Eve did some more stretching, getting herself ready when she heard the sound of raised voices from beyond the door.

Striding over to the door, Eve yanked it open just as Shane was saying. "This is unacceptable. We have signed contracts and you agreed to provide us with a fighter. You also should have given us adequate notice, so there was a chance for us to find a replacement if you weren't able to. You knew about this yesterday."

"What's going on?"

Andi looked at Shane and he nodded before continuing to glare at the other man.

"It would seem," Andi began, a serious expression on her face, "That the fighter from Belfast broke her wrist sparring yesterday and they couldn't get a replacement."

Eve cocked her hip against the door. "Well, okay. So what's the new plan?"

No one spoke for the longest time and the reality dawned on Eve. "No. Fuck this for a game of soldiers. I'm ready to fight. So I don't care what you have to do, hell, pick some feisty-looking woman from the crowd and let's go."

Eve stepped menacingly toward the short fat man, and the man held up his hands. "Hey, listen, I can't be held responsible for some wan breaking her wrist. I gave them an alternative and they said no. I did my best and look, if you can't or won't take it, then that's it. I obliged my contract."

What the hell was this dude on about?

"Hold up a damn minute. What alternative? I'm confused."

"Eve," Shane said softly, looking at her. "It isn't a viable option."

She arched her brow and gave him a hard glare. "How bout, you let me decide that for myself. My family is in the audience tonight. I can't just walk away."

Shane held her gaze, yet kept his lips firmly shut and Eve dragged her gaze from his to Andi. "Tell me."

"There is no female fighter available. One of the undercards had to cancel their fight because of sickness, so this idiot here thought that you wouldn't have a problem fighting him."

There wasn't a second that passed before Eve said. "I'll do it. I'll fight him."

"Like hell you will." Came Shane's growled response.

Ignoring Shane, and the horrified look on Andi's face, she looked at the promoter. "Tell your boy he's got a fight. The show must go on."

The man hurried away, and Eve strutted back into the room and took a drink of water. Shane stormed into the room, his face like thunder as he exploded. "Are you fucking insane? Do you have a death wish? You agreed to fight, and you didn't even ask about the other fighter? Don't you want to know his weight class? His stats? Fucking hell, Eve."

Eve ignored Shane's ramble. letting him growl and snarl until he said. "Fuck it. I'm calling it. My priority is keeping you safe and I can't condone this. I'm calling it off!"

Andi had come into the room, and her eyes darting back and forth between the two of them and when Shane made to go out the door, Eve had to stand in front of him, and she poked him in the chest. "You don't decide for me. I decide for me. And if you walk out that door and tell them that I am a coward and won't fight, I won't ever forgive you. My career is on the line. *Mine.* You fuck me over on this, Abercrombie, and I will sever ties with Rebel PR. I'll do it. Just like I'm going to fight in that Octagon, and you can't stop me!"

Their gazes locked in a silent battle of wills. Shane took a step toward her and for one moment, Eve didn't know if Shane wanted to kiss her, or hoist her over his shoulder and carry her out of the venue. Heartbeats passed and neither of them wanted to look away first.

In the end, it was Shane who looked away first, his expression resigned. "Fine, whatever. Do what you want. I can't stay here and watch it. I won't. *I can't.*"

"Right, well, fuck off then and let me get back to what I do. I'm sure Andi can find someone else to do the piss poor job that you've been doing managing me. So, bye, don't let the door hit you in the ass on the way out. I've got shit to do."

Shane stared at her for half a minute before he turned on his heels and barrelled his way past Andi, slamming the door shut on his way. Eve wanted to throw something she was so fucking mad at him for trying to tell her what to bloody do.

Eve turned to Andi, anger in her veins as she said. "Let's do this."

CHAPTER TWENTY-ONE

Shane

SHANE DIDN'T LEAVE. He couldn't.

He'd stormed out of the room fit to fucking strangle someone, but there was no way he could have left Eve to do this alone. If she was out of her mind and wanted to go ahead with this, he would just have to suck it up and shove down his concern to be there for her.

The last couple of days, Shane had felt better in himself than he had in a long time. Going to Little Leaps and finding the love he had for gymnastics hadn't been stolen from him by his dad had given him more than he had known he needed.

Shane had slipped back into it like he'd never been away, and even the last few days he'd slowly gone back to his routines of eating healthy and sleeping. He'd also managed to keep his bulimia in check and had even had a video call with his psychologist to talk about how he was feeling.

And Eve. He wanted to tell her everything because Shane wanted to try with her. He didn't want to have any secrets between them. Eve deserved to know all the horrid truth before she made up her mind on if she wanted to give them a shot.

Shane stood at the end of the entranceway where Eve would walk down before entering the cage, arms folded across his chest, and simmered with a nervous energy. He had always felt this sort of stillness before a competition, a calmness that had drowned out the world. But standing here, waiting for Eve to walk out...his stomach was tied up in a million knots.

"Ladies and Gentlemen, our next fight is a little unorthodox but sure to be an epic battle. First to enter the octagon, is your homegrown heroine, Eve Andrews!"

A gigantic roar almost tore the roof off the venue as the first bars of Eve's *Who's That Girl?* blared from the speakers and you almost, almost, couldn't hear it over the cheering. A spotlight suddenly flooded the walk away, and there she was.

Shane had seen her spar, he'd seen her in naked, but Eve had never looked fiercer than she did the moment the spotlight hit her. Eve's smile lit up the room and all eyes were on her. And so they should be. She rolled her shoulders, hood up as she strode down the walkway with so much swagger, it was undeniable that she was a presence.

She came to the end of the walkway, looked around and when her eyes landed on Shane, she blinked, then inclined her head to him. Eve flipped her hood down, then slipped her robe off and Shane couldn't stop himself from striding over and it from her.

Their fingers touched and Shane felt a bolt of electricity.

Then she was laser-focused again, walking over to the steps, shuffling her feet, and then she did some weird little fist thing where she hit her shoulders with a closed fist, then closed her eyes and muttered something before she went up and into the Octagon.

Shane had seen a few fights in his life. Been to a few UFC events. But nothing prepared him for Eve stepping into the cage and then scaling the fucking cage to sit on top of one of the corners and do a "Come on" with her hands.

Shane laughed despite his worry.

She was a badass.

"And her opponent, from Galway, Larry, the leprechaun, Canty!"

Drowning Pools *Let the bodies hit the floor* played as Shane looked down the walkway and his heart nearly leapt out of his chest. Eve's opponent was fucking huge, most likely well over six foot, with shoulders like battering rams. He looked like the Irish version of Brock Lesnar, except with ginger hair and a beard.

The only leprechaun thing about him was the tattoo on his chest.

This monster had to literally duck under the door of the cage.

Shane snapped his gaze to Eve. On the outside, she looked like the mammoth of a man didn't intimidate her in the slightest, but when she lifted her gaze to his, Shane saw a flicker of fear before she jumped down as this Larry stepped into the cage.

Eve looked like she was getting in a cage fight with Goliath.

Andi stepped beside him, her mouth nearly hanging open. "We need to stop this. I should have helped you stop this."

Shane shook his head. "Eve would only have dug her heels in more. She wouldn't have backed down. She would have gone in there regardless."

Larry the fucking leprechaun peered down at Eve and laughed, shaking his head.

Eve jerked her head up and smirked, nodded, and when the ref started the match, she went right in with a swift kick to hook the back of the man's knee with her foot which forced him down to kneel on it. Eve punched him square in the jaw, his head turning to the side, and blood spluttering from his mouth.

Shane hadn't been punched as hard as that, but Shane knew it had to have hurt.

Eve bounced back and went to kick him up side his head. But her foot never connected. A meaty hand grabbed Eve by the ankle and swung her, like she was a hurley. She crashed into the side of the cage. She was huddled over herself and slowly got to her feet. Shane could see blood on her face and a red mark on the side of her face from where she had hit the cage.

The other fighter was back on his feet and said something to Eve. He opened his arms, as if to taunt her. Eve lunged for him, alternating between punching and kicking as Larry laughed. Eve angled her body and did a flat-footed kick as hard as she could to the man's knee, and for a moment the Leprechaun's joint almost doubled back, and he went down again.

Eve put herself in danger by getting closer to him, and Shane started forward when the man's hand grabbed and caught Eve by the throat. Shane didn't think that was legal in any kind of fight. He watched as Eve used Larry's body to climb up and she wrapped her legs around his thick neck. She locked her ankles behind his head and twisted her body, all while the giant had his hand still around her throat.

Larry started to blink a couple of times, and Shane felt relief as he wondered if Eve might actually knock him out with that move. He lifted his other hand and punched Eve hard in the stomach, but she kept hanging in there. Then Larry brought his hand down again and again to no avail.

Shane could see when Larry was starting to fade. Eve had him on the ropes and was winning.

"Come on, baby. You have him."

"Baby?" Andi said with an amused smirk.

"Shut up, Collins." Shane mumbled, trying to stay focused on Eve.

Larry let out a curse, as if he knew that he was fading, then pulled on whatever reserve he had in the tank and swung his entire body and Eve toward the side of the cage. Her back hit it so hard the cage rattled, and then he slammed her again, and again until she let go and fell to the ground.

Eve was down and trying to get back up with Larry kicked her in the stomach, in the same spot that he'd punched a half dozen times. He kicked her once, twice, three times before reaching down to mash Eve's face against the cage.

He slapped her hard across the face, then stomped on Eve's head.

The referee stopped the fight and Larry had to be pulled back. Shane bolted toward the cage, pushing past everyone that was clambering to get a picture, and went straight to Eve. She wasn't moving. She was just lying there bleeding, her face a mess, and his heart was breaking.

"Eve, can you hear me?" Nothing. "Come on, baby. Open your eyes for me."

Her eyes fluttered. "Did I win?"

Her voice was slurred, and when she opened her eyes, they were glassy. She certainly had a concussion.

"Shane?"

"Ya, babe?" he said, glancing over his shoulder to see if the paramedics were coming.

"I like hearing you call me baby."

Shane looked back at Eve as her eyes rolled back in her head and she was out cold. Dread, cold, and fucking painful dread coiled in his stomach as paramedics shoved him out of the way and went to take a look at Eve. Shane tried to get them to tell him if Eve was okay, but no one was answering him.

A hand fell on his arm. "Let them work, Shane. Let them make sure she's okay."

"Fuck," he swore, dragging his hands in his hair. "I should have stopped it. I can't stand to see her like this...this is killing me."

Andi kept her hand on his arm as they brought in a stretcher and when Eve was rushed to the back for medical attention, Andi slipped her hand into his and he gripped onto her hand like his life depended on it.

Chapter Twenty-Two

Eve

Voices roused Eve from the dark pit she'd been beaten into.

She wished they would shut the hell up because they were wrecking her head.

Two men were arguing, and it made her head hurt more than it already was. Her face felt like she'd taken a hurley to it and as the details of the fight started coming back to her, Eve supposed she had. The moment that Larry the fucking leprechaun had strode down the walkway and into the cage, Eve had known that she was fucked. Royally so. Shane had been right, however there was no way in Hell Eve would ever, tell him that.

She might want to be naked with him again, but he'd be a smug prick if Eve gave him the impression that she should have listened to him and called off the fight. She'd be the laughingstock of the MMA community now because she'd lost and done so in her hometown.

"You are her manager. You should have fucking stopped

her front getting in there with that beast. You are responsible for this whether you own up to it or not."

Was that Darren?

"Do you know your cousin at all?" Came an angry snarl. Oh, it was definitely Darren out there. "The more you tell Eve she can't do something, the more she's gonna do it just to flip you off. I fucking tried. She told me to jog on. There was no talking her out of it."

Eve made to sit up but groaned as pain shot through her head. Putting her palm to her head, she took a deep breath before prying her eyes open. The light hurt her eyes and she grunted when she tried to swung her legs off whatever it was that she was laying on.

"Hey don't get up. You look like you're about to keel over." Darren said to her as he came over and gently helped her to sit upright, her legs hanging off the side of the bed. His hand was gentle as he put his fingers to her cheekbone, but when she hissed at the searing pain, he dropped his hand.

"He could have killed ya, Eve."

Eve snorted, then put her hand to her chest even though her entire body *ached*. "Still beating, cuz. I've taken harder hits from pint sized women. If it wasn't for the cheap shots, I'd have taken him. Don't think Larry's gonna make it in UFC if he's resorting to cheating to take out a woman like me."

Darren was looking at her like she was insane and then Eve suddenly remembered that her parents had witnessed it all and must be freaking the fuck out.

"Hey, Darren, can you go tell the parents that I'm grand and giving ya cheek. You know mam will calm down if you tell her. She always believes you."

Darren arched a brow. "So, you want me to lie?"

Eve grinned, then tried to hide her wince of pain. "Yes please."

Her cousin huffed out an exaggerated sigh, then kissed her forehead. "I'll see you in a bit."

Eve watched as Shane and Darren glared at one another, turning the air frigid and thick with tension before Darren yanked open the door and walked out, just as Andi ducked inside and closed the door behind her. Andi and Shane shared a look, then Andi turned to Eve, while Shane leaned against the wall with his arms across his chest.

He looked like the reigns on his temper were about to snap.

"Well, the promoter has had his ass handed to him by me, and I threatened to blacklist him and all his stupidity with all the PR companies I could think of for this clusterfuck. You get the prize money and the win, which I know will please you."

Eve slid her gaze from Andi to Shane, his jaw clenched so tight it had to hurt. The dizziness was starting to lessen, and she no longer felt like she was gonna upchuck all over the floor. That was progress, right?

"What are people saying? Am I a joke now?"

Andi snorted, shaking her head. "Far from it. I've just had a few mangers come up to me saying their fighters, their *female* fighters, want a fight. Both mine and Shane's phones have been blowing up. Big money's been thrown around. You need to take it easy for a couple of days and then we can all sit down and look at options."

Eve felt her lips curve into a smile. This was good. This was really good. More offers meant more of a profile so the beating she'd taken today wouldn't have slowed down her momentum.

Andi looked over her shoulder and Eve looked back at Shane again. "You got anything to say about it all?"

There was a moment of utter silence before Shane replied in a cold and emotionless tone. "Like you'd fucking listen to my opinion anyways."

Her smile fell. The come down from the fight was slowly spreading through her and she was angry and tired and just fucking sick of it all. Eve could almost feel Shane judging her, sensing that he was seeing how she looked now, after the fight, bruised and battered, and that was all he saw.

That was all that people saw in the end. They didn't see the hours of training. The practice. The studying that went into perfecting her craft. The moment she got a black eye or a bruised rib or some shit, the opinion changed. And Eve fucking hated that.

She pushed off the bed, got to her feet and tried to ignore the room spinning. She took the wraps off her hands and tossed them to the side. Eve grabbed a towel and wiped the sweat from her skin before she addressed Andi.

"Can you give us a minute?"

Andi shook her head. "Um, I don't think that's the best plan. You both look like you are ready to embark on round two and considering your cousin and my employee already almost came to blows, I have to act as an intermediary."

Eve glared at Shane, who just stared back with cold eyes, and said nothing.

Fine, whatever. Eve had no problem throwing down with Andi in the room.

"Right, well, since Abercrombie needs a babysitter, I think it's best that we have someone else manage my career."

"You're the client. You can't order us fucking around." Shane ground out through gritted teeth.

"It's not an order, dickhead. It's a condition of continuing my contract with Rebel PR. I can see it on your face that you can't handle me fighting so I want a new manager."

"That wasn't a fucking fight!" Shane snapped, his voice raising as Andi tried to get in between them and Shane shook his head. "That was fucking stupidity and hubris and insanity all rolled into one. He could have killed you because you were trying to prove a goddamn point!"

Eve gave him a hard stare. "I won, didn't I?"

Shane snorted in response. "Ya, don't think you can celebrate a win when the only reason you won was because he cheated. That's not something celebrate, Eve."

Maybe it was the condescending tone. Maybe it was the look of arrogance on his stupid handsome face, but Eve wanted to deck him and break his nose for real this time. But instead of using her fists, Eve took her shot with her words.

"Like I'm gonna take advice from a washed up has been like you. I saw the hopper you took at the Olympics, and you just quit. One fall and you were done. We might have fucked, Abercrombie, but that does not mean you get to lecture me about what I choose to do with my life or my career. You can go fuck yourself and run away. From all accounts, you're damn good at that."

Nothing happened for a hot minute, but Eve saw the moment her words slapped him across the face like she'd physically struck him. Shane's entire body tensed, his chest rising and falling in rapid succession and there was something in his eyes that Eve wanted to take it all back, her heart clenching.

Andi's eyes darted from Eve to Shane as she opened her mouth to say something, but Shane just shook his head, shoved off the wall, then opened the door and walked out without saying another word.

He closed the door softly behind him, but the finality of it was so fucking loud that it sounded like a gunshot had gone off and the bullet was aimed right at her fucking chest where her heart was breaking.

Eve couldn't believe that Shane had just walked away. He hadn't even tried to fight and to stay there with her and now, hot, fat, tears spilled out of her eyes and Eve wanted to scream. Instead, she grabbed the nearest chair and ignoring the agony in her body, flung it at the wall before she buried her face in her hands, the enormity of the night weighing down on her.

"Eve, are you okay?" Andi asked her, but, Eve couldn't answer her.

No, she wasn't okay...she was the opposite of fucking okay.

Chapter Twenty-Three

Shane

"*Like I'm gonna take advice from a washed up has been like you. I saw the hopper you took at the Olympics, and you just quit. One fall and you were done. We might have fucked, Abercrombie, but that does not mean you get to lecture me about what I choose to do with my life or my career. You can go fuck yourself and run away. From all accounts, you're damn good at that.*"

Eve's words had been banging around in his head since the fight a couple of days ago and he'd walked out of the venue, headed home, and started packing his stuff up. He couldn't stay here. He couldn't.

And he never should have let his defences down and let himself develop feelings for Eve. Like, how stupid was he to even think that someone like her, someone who never backed down from a fight, would ever want to be with a man who had been a coward his entire life.

Shane had been a coward when he'd been unable to stand up to his dad. He'd been a coward when the doctors told him that his shoulder was healed enough to go back to gymnastics, and he'd just quit. Shane knew he had been a coward when he had run away from Ireland to Manchester and an even worse coward when he allowed his eating disorder to control him.

Andi had come over and begged him to stay. Andrea Collins never begged anyone, and she begged him to stay and work things out, so he had agreed reluctantly. Andi had given Eve a week off to recuperate, then they would meet when tempers were less frayed. Eve and Shane hadn't spoken since the argument after the fight and despite living across the hall from one another, they'd not bumped into one another either.

Shane had not gone back to Little Leaps since the morning of the fight. He didn't feel like he deserved the happiness that he felt when he was there, so he just stopped going.

He supposed that made him an even bigger coward.

Shane had tried to go for a run this morning, but had felt dizzy, his heartbeat erratic. He'd barely eaten anything since Friday and anything he did eat came right back up. It was strange that the one thing that made Shane feel like he had control over himself was the prime example of how out of control he really was.

Ronan was back in Cork and had been pestering him for days to meet up. Shane knew if he kept blowing him off, then Ronan would get suspicious of him, then come, and check up on him. If he came to see Shane and Shane wasn't prepared, then there was no way he'd be able to convince Ronan that he was okay, and not in the midst of another relapse.

Shane shouldn't have listened to Andi when she begged him.

He should have gotten the first available flight back to Manchester.

Shane managed to swallow down a cereal bar and drink a shake this morning so he wouldn't look pale or give anything away. It had taken every ounce of willpower not to vomit it all back up. Shane had borrowed a car from Andi's brother Rhys, and he parked the car in the car park beside Rebel Ink, hoping he wouldn't bump into Eve's cousin Darren.

Locking the car, Shane pulled out his phone to text Ronan so he could come down from the apartment he now shared in an exclusive complex down the road from where his fiancée worked. He was distracted from messaging Ronan by a work email that came into his inbox and he wasn't paying his usual attention to his surroundings.

His shoulder bumped into someone, and Shane drew his head up to apologize when he froze, unable to move as ever instinct in his body urged him to keep walking.

Henry Carter looked the same as he always had, except that his hair now had streaks of grey. His dad's eyes were wide when he realized that it was Shane standing in front of him and when Henry reached out to rest a hand on his arm, Shane recoiled, backing away.

"When did you come back?"

The first words Henry had spoken to him in eight years, and they were said in an accusatory tone, like Shane should have given his dad a heads up that he dared come back to Cork. Shane's heart was racing, and he couldn't quash the fear that iced his veins.

The woman standing beside him eyed Shane with curiosity, like she was trying to figure out who Shane was.

"You lose your tongue too, lad, as well as your dignity when you fucked off to be with the Brits?"

"No, I just don't waste words on people who don't deserve them." Shane snapped, unable to catch the words before he said them out loud.

His dad laughed, a mocking sound. "Ah, so still a cheeky little shit then. Eight years since I've seen ya and not even a pleasant word for your father?"

The woman with his dad looked shocked to realize that Shane was Henry's son. Shane didn't respond to Henry, just looked at him and all the feelings, all the emotions that Shane had locked away in a box came rushing back.

"I see you've been working with that female PR company. I suppose it's the best job for you considering you were always a little bitch, right? Taking orders from women when you could have been a fucking superstar. Pathetic as always, lad."

Shane couldn't respond, his retort lodged in his throat as his dad slung his arm around the shoulders of the woman. She kind of flinched when he did it, and Shane wondered had his dad's abusive nature spread to the woman he was dating.

"You were my greatest failure. But we have a daughter now and she's even better than you were at her age at gymnastics. Works hard. Doesn't give me shit. Does what she's told. She knows that a gold medal is the objective, and our girl would never be happy to settle for a first loser's medal."

Shane felt sick. He had a sister. He had a sister that Henry was free to abuse again.

Shane shifted his gaze to the woman. "Take your daughter and run. Don't look back. Don't make the fucking mistake my mother made and leave her with him. He doesn't care about her. He will taunt and tear her down until she is nothing but a shell of a person."

Henry went to grab for him but Shane sidestepped him and continued to speak to this sister's mother. "He will control her because of what he wants. Does she avoid eating meals with you? Does she count calories and get anxious when she eats too much? Because that's what he did to me. I didn't give up the sport I love because of an injury...it was to get away from the monster who made me bulimic."

Recognition flared in the woman's eyes, and she slapped away Henry's hands when he reached for her. Then she walked away without looking back and Shane was relieved. He'd never have forgiven himself if he'd let Henry ruin another child.

"You bastard!" Henry roared at him, drawing attention from onlookers. "You pathetic, piss poor excuse of a person. Weak, that's what you are. I gave you fucking everything, and what you blame me for is the woman's illness that you did to yourself." Henry grabbed hold of his hoodie and dragged Shane closer. "You can blame me all you want. You can. But you will always be a disappointment to everyone around you. I wish I'd smothered you when you were born, lad."

His dad shoved him away then, and Shane stumbled, landing on his ass on the ground as Henry stormed off after the woman. He sat there, unable to move for a moment until an older lady asked him if he was okay.

Getting to his feet, Shane turned round and stalked back to the car. Panic flared inside him, and he couldn't breathe or get his heart rate to calm down. Taking out his phone with hands that trembled, he texted Ronan and told him that something had come up at work and he couldn't meet up.

Resting his head on the steering wheel, Shane knew his dad was right. He was weak. He couldn't blame his dad for his eating disorder because at the end of the day, Shane had been the one to do that to himself. Shane had been the one to decide to purge his food to compensate for any extra food he might eat.

Henry might have been the catalyst, but Shane was the pathetic child who had followed through.

Shane drove the car to the nearest garage, filled a couple of bags with as much junk food as he could, and then drove Rhys's car back to the apartment. Once in the confines of his apartment, Shane ripped the bags open, alternating between stuffing his face and opening another bag, then another, then another, trying to fill the gaping hole in his chest.

Chapter Twenty-Four

Eve

Eve had taken the last week off to allow for her body to mend and to put some distance between her and Shane. She had half expected him to reach out to her, maybe apologise, but she'd only gotten radio silence. The only inclination that he was still even in the country was because when Andi had sent the invite to the meeting for today, Shane had been included in the email and had responded with an – I'll be there.

She'd spent the last week crashing at Darren's, flirting with Cathal, and making him squirm even as his girlfriend laughed and teased him. She'd had meals with her parents, once she'd been able to put make-up on her face without pain making her eyes water. It had been a good break from everything, but now she was ready to get back to it.

And Eve had decided that she needed to say sorry to Shane. He didn't deserve the awful things she'd said to him in the heat of the moment. Over the past couple of days, Eve had considered texting him her apology, and yet, she thought better of it, knowing that would be the coward's way out. She would swallow her pride and apologise and maybe, just maybe, salvage something from the wreckage of that night.

On her first night staying with Darren, his girlfriend Nessa had come over for dinner. Eve watched as Darren kissed and teased his girlfriend as they dished out the takeout, and Eve was delighted that her cousin had found someone who really made him that happy.

Nessa had come over and handed Eve her plate, then looked at Eve with an amused expression before she asked Eve what had Eve looking at her with a serious expression.

Nessa sat down on the couch opposite her, curling her legs underneath her, taking the drink Darren handed to her before he went back over to the kitchen area. Eve was still staring at her, and Nessa flushed. "Do I have something in my teeth or what?"

Eve chuckled. "No. Sorry. When Darren told me that he was in love with the woman from the bookshop, I wondered how he'd managed to convince you to date him. I mean, you guys are complete opposites and even people who have a shit ton in common can't make it work."

Nessa smiled, the expression making her look even more beautiful. "He was kind to me. Darren was patient with me and didn't shy away from the darkness I carried with me. He made me laugh, and I was in love with him before I even realised it." Darren came to flop down beside his girlfriend, and grinned as he started to eat his food.

"And the amazing sex. Don't forget to compliment me on the sex."

Eve laughed as Nessa went bright red and smacked him on the arm, only to freeze, like for a second she was waiting for him to retaliate. Eve knew that Nessa's psycho ex had beaten her within an inch of her life, had berated her, and terrified the other woman, and Eve wanted five minutes in a cell with him to see how he fared against a woman who wasn't afraid to hit back.

Eve just observed as Darren noted her hesitation, reached over, and grabbed a spring roll off Nessa's plate, kissed her cheek, and pretended like Nessa had never even contemplated that Darren would strike her.

Nessa sheepishly took a drink from her glass, then dropped her gaze to her food.

Darren met Eve's gaze and shook his head a little, telling Eve to leave it, and Eve would. The poor girl had enough trauma over the years that her gut reaction wasn't her fault. Nessa had made a lot of strides since her ex went to prison, but she still had more steps to do.

"I dunno, cuz. I still can't believe you managed to get a good-looking woman to date you. I mean, you defo punching above your weight class with Nessa."

Darren grinned. "I know. Strokes my ego though. And I really do like it when she stro-"

"Finish that sentence Darren Fitzgerald and I swear to gods, the only thing that will be stroking you is your own damn hand."

Eve burst out laughing at the horrified expression on Nessa's face when she finished, and then she smiled and laughed with Eve, as poor Darren pretended to look insulted. And just like that the tone of the evening changed and Eve knew that Darren would one day marry Nessa.

Some people were just meant to be together.

Eve had spent a lot of time thinking about things the last couple of days and she realised that she missed spending time with Shane. She missed teasing him and even after one very hot and sexy day, she missed who he was when he didn't look so damn haunted.

She wasn't in love with him yet, but she was close to falling over the last hurdle.

If she could make him accept her apology that is.

Eve walked over to the Rebel PR offices, a nervous anxiety making her jittery. She walked in and her heart sank a little to see only Andi in the office. She was talking to someone on her computer, and she held up her hand to tell Eve to give her five minutes. Eve went into Shane's office and damn her girlie heart that the moment she caught his scent, she felt a little giddy on the inside.

She plonked herself down on his chair and twirled around, hoping that Andi finished her call and Shane rocked up soon, wanting to get the business talk out of the way so she could talk to Shane in private and tell him how she felt.

Andi finished up her call and came to lean in the doorway of Shane's office. She had this expression on her face that made Eve's stomach sink. "He's not coming, is he?"

"He said he would. I tried calling him when he missed an earlier meeting and Charlie tried him but got no answer. I texted Ronan too. Shane has never missed a meeting in his life."

"Is it because of me?" Eve blurted out.

Andi looked sad as she shrugged. "I don't know. I forced him to come back here, and he hasn't been himself since. And now, on top of everything, I have to deal with a contract issue that just came up. Would you go over and knock at his apartment and just check on him? I can't shake the feeling that something's wrong."

Eve got to her feet. "Sure. I don't know if he will answer if it's me, but I'll give it a shot. Do I need to break the door down and make sure he's okay?"

"I hope not. I'm staying around here for the next couple of hours so give me a shout if he opens the door to you. Might stop me and Charlie stressing like mother hens."

Eve nodded, then walked out and crossed the industrial estate to the apartments. She went up on the elevator, her leg bouncing as she wondered if Shane would open the door to her. Eve strode right up to the door and knocked once.

Nothing.

She knocked again and then called out. "Shane? It's Eve."

Still nothing.

"Hey look, I know you probably don't want to talk to me, but Andi's worried. Hell, I'm worried. Can you just open the door so I don't feel like a right bell end and am talking to myself out in the hall?"

The elevator pinged and Eve hoped it was Shane who came striding out, but it wasn't Shane who came out. Eve knew Ronan Cusack, Shane's best friend, from the media, and of course she knew his fiancée, Sorcha Healy, who was part owner of Rebel Books with Niamh Kent. Darren had introduced them a couple of weeks ago. Ronan had a very serious expression on his face, and Eve knew the other man was worried about his friend.

"I tried knocking but he didn't answer," Eve told them. "You think he's gone back to Manchester? I'm Eve by the way."

"Hey," Ronan said, shaking his head. "I checked in with his college friends and no one's seen him. He wouldn't go without telling me. Don't ask me how I know but I do."

Sorcha squeezed Ronan's hand before he let go and knocked on the door. "Shane, it's me. Open the door or I'm gonna kick it down and then kick your ass for stressing me out."

Still nothing.

Ronan pulled out his phone, and dialled Shane's number and a moment later, a phone rang inside the apartment. It rang and rang before going to voicemail.

"Goddammit, Shane," Ronan mumbled before he looked at the door, shaking his head. "Fuck this shit."

Ronan lifted his foot and kicked the door. It didn't budge,

just made a loud sound, and then he did it again and again. There was a dent in the door now, but they weren't any closer to getting inside. Ronan looked shaken and was about to kick it again when Eve stopped him.

"It needs a little more force. Shoulder it. On the count of three. One. Two. Three."

CHAPTER TWENTY-FIVE

Eve

THE DOOR BURST open with the combined force of their shoulders and Ronan stumbled forward. Eve grabbed the back of his jacket to stop him from face-planting. She released his jacket when he looked like he had his balance back. The look of fear on his face made Eve want to know what Ronan knew that Eve didn't.

Was he worried that Shane might do something to hurt himself?

"Shane? Where are ya?"

Sorcha came into the apartment and walked over to the living room and that was when Eve saw the absolute mess. Empty packets of crisps, empty chocolate bars, and discarded packets of eaten sweets and biscuits all lay around the place and when Eve looked from the chaos to Ronan, his face was pale, and he looked shook.

"What is it?"

Ronan took off down the hall, leaving Eve and Sorcha to

follow him. Coming to a halt at the door to the bathroom, Ronan let out a curse before he said. "Ah, no. Ah, buddy."

Eve pushed past Sorcha and then it was her who came to a halt in the doorway. She saw Shane's body slumped against the wall space between the shower and the toilet, his eyes closed as Ronan got down on the ground and pulled his friend to him.

"Shane. It's me, mate. Open your eyes for me. Come on now. Don't do this to me again."

Again? Do this again? What the hell was Ronan on about?

"I'll call an ambulance," Sorcha said softly.

"No."

Everyone let out a sigh of relief at the pained sound that had come from Shane's lips. She wanted to go to him, and check he was okay, but after Ronan's comment, Eve trusted that his best friend knew what was best for him.

Shane slumped toward Ronan, resting his head on the other man's shoulder. "I fucked up."

Wrapping an arm around his friend, Ronan shook his head. "No. You stumbled. I hate to tell ya this Shane Carter, but you're only human."

Shane didn't respond to Ronan's teasing though his body shuddered, and a few minutes later, Sorcha came in with a blanket and handed it to Ronan. He draped it over Shane's body, and Eve was shocked at how small he looked, how fragile.

She was totally confused as to what the hell was wrong with him.

Ronan brushed the sweat-laden hair from Shane's face. "You gonna tell me what happened?"

"No."

Ronan chuckled, and Eve was surprised to see a smile curve his lips. "Then maybe I'll sic Sorcha on ya. I think she'd get it out of you."

"You know I'm a straight shooter, Shane."

Shane flinched at the sound of Sorcha's voice. "Oh god, you told her."

Sorcha edged past Eve to lower herself onto the floor. "No. Ronan hasn't told me anything. I promise. I wish he had so I'd understand what's happening. Or you could tell me."

"No."

The sound came out with more pain than Eve had ever heard before and she sucked in a breath. It was the wrong thing to do because Shane curled into himself. "Oh god, everyone will know. Leave me alone. I just want to be left alone."

His words were slurred, like he was drunk or something, and Eve would be pissed if that was the case. Was Shane some alcoholic who had gotten himself smashed and was now dealing with the consequences? Had he fallen off the wagon and this was what Ronan had to deal with before?

Ronan must have realized that Eve was starting to add things up in her head, and he shook his head, before he focused on his friend again. He pulled Ronan as close as he could, then reached down to take Shane's hand, but his eyes stayed locked with Eve's, like he was about to unburden himself.

Eve could never have expected what was about to be revealed.

"Shane, mate, when was the last time you ate? Not the shite outside but had a proper meal?"

"Fuck off, Ronan."

Ronan chuckled softly. "You being a grumpy bastard hasn't scared me off yet, cause yeah, that doesn't work with me. So, you know I'll keep asking till you tell me."

"Friday, okay. Fucking Friday."

The day of the fight. Why the fuck wouldn't he have eaten since then?

"How long have you been slipping?"

Shane kept his eyes shut and pressed his lips together. When he didn't answer, Ronan sighed. "That long, eh? Okay, we've been down this road before. We can do this. We need to call Carla and you need to tell me what made you slip?"

So, Ronan was an alcoholic?

Shane refused to answer so Ronan brushed his thumb along Shane's forehead like he was comforting him. "I'm gonna start making assumptions here, buddy, so stop me if I'm wrong, okay?" Shane still said nothing, so Ronan carried on. "Being back here dragged you into the past. It reminded you of all the shite that fucking bastard put you through. You didn't feel in control, and you fell back on old habits."

A tear slipped down Shane's cheek, making her chest ache as Eve lowered herself to the ground, and hugged her knees to her chest. She leaned on her knees and couldn't look at Sorcha who was also trying not to cry.

"I saw him."

Ronan flinched. "When?"

"Yesterday. I have a sister. I think he's doing the same to her. I told her mam to get her away from him. She believed me. But he already broke me, Ronan. She can be fixed but I'm a lost cause."

Jesus Christ...had someone abused Shane?

"It must have been a shock to see your dad after eight years. No wonder you slipped."

"I'm weak and pathetic. Just like he always said."

Eve's heart was shattering, breaking into a million different pieces for the man so ravaged by whatever had happened to him as a child. She wanted to find the person who hurt Shane and make him bleed. She wanted to hurt him as much as he'd made his son hurt.

"You had no one to protect you when your mam left, Shane. You were a child. You were a child whose father punished him if he was late for training. You were a child whose dad watched everything you ate. You were a teenager when your dad made you compete in the Olympics knowing his excessive training had fucked your shoulder."

Shane shuddered again, and Ronan went on. "You were a child when your dad broke your nose, and when he almost gave you pneumonia because he made you run so many laps for being late back from my house that you vomited and then he hosed you down, making you train soaked to the skin."

Some fucking people didn't deserve to be parents. They really didn't.

"You made the decision to walk away from the sport you loved to stay alive. You worked hard to forge a new life for yourself, and you were well for so long, Shane. So fucking long."

Shane didn't respond for the longest time, and they just sat there in silence until she heard Shane say. "I can't get my heart to stop racing. My meds didn't work, and I vomited them up. I feel like I'm dying."

Ronan chuckled softly, and Eve marvelled at how he could be so calm, when Eve was fucking raging.

"You're not dying, your body's just not best pleased with you at the moment. You need a doctor." Ronan told Shane.

"No hospital. They won't let me out. Please. No hospital."

Ronan brushed his forehead again. "Okay, no hospital. But you have to get checked out."

When Shane didn't argue, Ronan lifted his eyes to Sorcha, and even saw the sheen of wetness in his eyes. "Healy, will you call Andi and ask her if she has a discreet doctor who can come have a look at Shane. Will you tell her that he has a heart arrhythmia and his pills haven't returned it to its normal rhythm? Will you tell her that he is most likely to be dehydrated due to lack of fluids, and that the arrhythmia is a side effect of an eating disorder?"

Eve felt like she had been hit by a truck. What the hell was

Ronan talking about? She had seen Shane naked. He looked spectacular and muscular and fit and healthy. He didn't have an eating disorder...he didn't.

Shane let loose a pained groan, and Ronan pulled him closer. "It's okay. I've got you. I've always got you. We had a slip, and we can take control again. Did you eat all that stuff and then purge it all again?"

Eve thought of the things she had said to Shane when she was angry, and she hated herself a little now that she knew the truth. She understood now why Shane had bolted when she'd suggested they go for breakfast after they hooked up. He'd been in the middle of a relapse and Eve had made it all worse.

Chapter Twenty-Six

Shane

SHANE NODDED HIS HEAD MUTELY, feeling embarrassed and betrayed. "You told them. You promised you wouldn't. You promised you'd never tell anyone I have bulimia. You fucking lied."

"I had to, Shane. You can hate me all you want but at least you'll be alive to do it. You'll be alive to do it. Sorcha, call Andi please."

His career was over. Andi and Charlie would think him unstable and fire him. He'd ruined the career he had built because he had been weak and let himself revert back to hurting himself.

"Andi, stop asking me questions I can't answer and just do what I fucking told you. Also, you might want to call someone to fix the door because Eve and Ronan broke it trying to get in."

Sorcha hung up and grumbled. "Jesus, that woman is not used to having people give her orders. Guess Deco likes it. I wonder if she tells him what to do in bed too."

Shane couldn't help himself, he laughed, and the moment he did, he felt Ronan relax against him. His friend had been calm on the outside, but Shane had known that he was anything but on the inside. They'd travelled down this road before. Shane despised himself for making Ronan suffer with him.

Pathetic excuse for a man. Weak ass bitch.

Shane rubbed at his chest as his heart squeezed and Ronan told him to take a few deep breaths. He did as he was told, and it helped but Shane was fucking ashamed to have everyone was seeing him like this. Since coming home yesterday, he'd spent the day alternating between eating and purging. He'd started to feel unwell and then he'd passed out in the bathroom.

"Eve, will you run into the kitchen and grab some 7-up for Shane?"

"Ugh, sure. Ya, no hassle."

When she was gone, Ronan said. "Right, now that the girl you like is gone, you wanna try and get up? Might be an idea to have more room when the doc comes. You think you can stand?"

Shane wasn't really sure of anything right now, but he nodded. It took him an awful long time before he could persuade his limbs to work, and even at that, it was only Ronan who kept him upright. He hoisted Shane up and walked with him to the bedroom when Shane said he couldn't face the carnage in the living room.

It was too embarrassing.

Ronan helped him to the bed, then sat down on the end of it as Eve came in with the 7-up. She hesitated in the door-way, only moving when Ronan asked her if she wanted him to take it. Shane kept his head down as he reached out and took the glass from Eve.

"Thanks."

"No hassle. You need anything else?"

Ya, he thought. I need you to go back to fighting with me. I need you to look at me like I'm a man and not a pathetic excuse of a man who has a fucking eating disorder. I need to know that this doesn't change how you feel about me.

Shane just shook his head, then set the glass down, pulling his knees to his chest and resting his forehead on his knees. He heard raised voices in the living room, and Ronan got to his feet, asking Eve to sit with him while he went to check on things.

He felt the bed shift as Eve sat down, but she didn't say anything for the longest time.

"You don't have to babysit me," he told her, knowing this must be the last thing she wanted to do. "You can head off."

"I'm grand where I am, Abercrombie. I was gonna apologise for being such a bitch to you, but now's not the time. You deserve to know I mean it and I'm not feeling sorry for ya."

Shane snorted. "It's grand. It's not like anything's gonna happen between us now. I fucked that up."

"Apart from the pale skin, you still look good to me, Abercrombie. I'd not say no to some naked gymnastics again. Oh shite, that's inappropriate, isn't it?"

Shane gave her a smile and then opened his eyes to look at Eve, expecting to see her face full of pity. Instead, he saw compassion and understanding in her eyes. "Yano, it makes me feel somewhat normal you not sugarcoating your words to me."

"You are normal, Shane. You just had a shitty upbringing and were faced with your abuser. I wish you'd told me about your bulimia, so I'd have understood." Eve glanced toward the door where the raised voices grew louder. "Is this why you freaked out when I said we'd go for breakfast? Because you'd relapsed and didn't want me to know?"

Shane snorted, shaking his head. "Pathetic, right?"

"No. Not in the slightest."

Shane heard the belief in her tone, and he wanted to cling to it, to make himself believe. He opened his mouth to speak but then Andi was standing in the doorway, followed by Ronan and Sorcha. His best friend didn't look best pleased as he glared at Andi.

"I can't believe you hid this from me. I can't believe you didn't tell me or Charlie."

Shane lifted his eyes to Andi's. "Because I didn't want you to look at me like you are now, Collins. I wanted you to take the piss out of me, to order me about, and think I'd do what you wanted without seeing me as broken. Just like you do now."

Andi didn't answer him, and Shane put his fists to his temples.

"Say something to him," Ronan growled, and Shane loved his best friend for trying to protect him. "Don't just fucking stand there after he told you that. You wanna know what happened? Ask him. He's not fucking broken, Andi, no matter what he thinks."

"Ronan, it's grand." Shane told him, but obviously, Ronan was not done.

"No, it's not fucking grand, Shane. It's far from it. Andi can't just come in without knowing all the facts and making stupid assumptions. She doesn't know the goddamn facts so I'm gonna tell her."

Shane opened his eyes to see Ronan glaring at Andi. "His dad was a controlling, manipulative bastard who pushed and pushed his son until something had to give. The broken nose, the bruises from the slaps, the forcing an eight-year-old to count fucking calories wasn't enough. He verbally ran him down on the daily, tearing away his confidence and his sense of self-worth until all Shane believed was that the only thing he could be loved for was a gold fucking medal. That was the only thing his dad cared about so don't you dare look at him like that. You're supposed to be his bloody friend for fuck sake."

Ronan sank his hands into his hair and turned away, Sorcha going to place her hand on his shoulder. Jesus, he'd done that to Ronan, his normally calm and collected friend didn't lose his temper that often, and Shane hated that he had done this to him.

Infecting everyone with your weakness, aren't ya lad?

"I don't think you're broken." Andi finally said quietly. "I'm just so mad at you for not telling me. I could have helped you. We could have supported you and if I had known, I'd never have pushed so hard for you to come back here. But I don't agree with this no hospital thing. If you have some issues with your heart, then maybe you should be checked in a hospital. They have people there that can help with your...your..."

"It's not a dirty word, Collins. You can't catch it by saying it. I have bulimia. I'm bulimic and I've had a relapse. But I can get through it, and it won't effort my work."

Andi threw her hands up in the air. "I'm not worried about that, you idiot. I'm worried about you. From what they've told me, you could have killed yourself. Maybe the best thing is to call an ambulance and have you held for seventy-two hours for being a danger to yourself."

Now Shane was angry. He glared at Andi. "You do that, and I swear the moment I'm discharged, you'll never see me again. I'll leave Cork and I won't go back to Manchester. I swear, Collins, I'll do it."

Andi held his glare for a moment before she rubbed at her chest. "I know you would you stubborn asshole. I'm trying to understand but none of it makes sense. I need to understand."

Ya, Shane thought he needed to understand why he did this to himself as well.

A knock sounded and everyone looked at the door as the man introduced himself as Connor Walsh, a paramedic and

Andi's future brother-in-law. He ignored everyone else and went straight to Shane and reached out and touched him on the shoulder.

"Can I give ya the once over so Collins over there doesn't burst a blood vessel? My brother's fond of her and it would make things a hell of a lot easier for me?"

Shane started to panic, then felt a hand slip into his. He looked up at Eve, who smiled. "I'm here. Everyone can leave and it will just be me, you, and Connor. Sound good?"

CHAPTER TWENTY-SEVEN

Shane

SHANE WAS TRYING HARD NOT to panic. His dad had been very selective in the doctors he chose to look at Shane if he had an injury, or if Henry had done something to hurt Shane, and then when he'd had his fall, the doctors had sussed that he had an eating disorder and they'd sent him to that treatment facility. Andi was already threatening to put him on a psych hold and the paramedic was her future brother-in-law, so Shane didn't like his chances.

Lifting his eyes to Ronan, his friend gave him a reassuring smile. "The rest of us will just be outside. You can shout if you need us. That okay?"

Shane nodded and Ronan ushered Sorcha and Andi out.

"Ronan?" Shane said, making his friend stop. "Thank you."

Ronan grinned. "Need my best man healthy and happy, don't I?"

Shane laughed and it eased some of the tension as Ronan closed the door and Connor stayed where he was until Shane gave him a nod. Connor chatted away about everything and anything as he examined Shane, rambling on about TV shows, movies, and music. Shane knew he was trying to put Shane at ease, and it helped a little, though he was still worried that Connor would tell him that he really needed to be in hospital.

After ten long minutes, two of which Connor just listened to his heart, he slung his stethoscope around his neck and pulled a chair over toward the bed. Shane took a sip of the 7-up Eve had brought in for him and waited as Connor leaned back in his chair and rested one leg on the other.

"Right, well the good news, Shane, is that your arrhythmia has settled, and heartrate has slowed to normal. You know it was probably a result of the excessive purging." Shane felt his cheeks heat in embarrassment, but Connor just started talking again like he didn't notice.

"Your throat is a little pissed off with you right now, so I'm gonna ask you to try and take in some fluids. Declan swears by hot Tanora and some honey when his throat is giving him hassle. I'm pretty sure he adds whisky to it, although, I'd leave that out for a while. Other than that, physically, you are not quite okay, but you'll be grand."

Shane was waiting for the next part, the mental part of the equation.

"I can almost see the wheels turning in your head. I'm not a psychologist and I think you've got more experience with your eating disorder than I do. Can I ask how long you've lived it?"

Shane scrubbed a hand down his face. "Officially, they diagnosed me after the Olympics. My dad had been pressuring me the week before and I'd binged and purged the night before and my shoulder, it was already iffy. After the fall, and when I went to the treatment place, they said my issues with food must have started when I was like seven or eight. That's when my dad started making me count my calories."

"Fucking prick," Eve growled and Shane squeezed her hand.

Connor blinked, like he couldn't believe what Shane had told him. "I agree with your girlfriend, your Da's a prick. Did you want to kill yourself this time? Sorry to be blunt but it's the paramedic in me, really needing to know."

Shane shook his head, not wanting to correct Connor when he assumed Eve was his girlfriend. "No, I swear. I felt like I had no control. It's always that. When I feel like even when everything else is out of my control I can control what I do to my body. It's stupid that the one thing I could control is the one thing that wrecks me."

"Not stupid, mate. Totally understandable. It's a learned behaviour. And because your prick of a Da forced you to hide it, you never got the help to try and unlearn it."

Shane raised a brow. "I thought you weren't a shrink?"

Connor grinned and Shane could see the family resemblance then. "Dated a psychology student once, something must have rubbed off on me."

Getting to his feet, Connor shoved his hands into his pocket. "Right, I'm gonna head out since I can confirm that you're grand. Can I ask a favour though?"

Shane shrugged his shoulders, feeling a little apprehensive. "Sure."

"Get my number off Andi. You don't feel well, or your heart starts playing silly beggars again, you call me. Hell, if you feel like you want to talk to someone on the outside, call me. I like to follow up with my patients, but if you're sticking around in Cork, it would be nice to have someone to tell me all the dirty secrets about what Collins got up to in Manchester for the wedding speech."

Connor walked out as Shane laughed, winking at Eve as he closed the door, leaving them alone. Shane wasn't sure what to say now that he was alone with Eve. How do you start to explain to the first woman you had serious feelings for just how much your dad fucked you up."

"You want me to run out and get some Tanora and honey like Connor said? Or I could send one of the others."

"Not right now, but thanks," Shane replied, then lifted his gaze to Eve's. "You don't have to stay now. I bet the last thing you were expecting when we hooked up was that you'd feel obligated to babysit me."

"Shut up ya idiot. I'm here cause I wanna be. I mean, as your girlfriend, I'm all in."

Shane ran a hand through his hair. "Connor just assumed. I should have corrected him."

Eve lifted her brow, pursing her lips. "Are you breaking up with me, Shane Carter?"

"Eve," Shane started, sitting up in the bed. "I don't know how to do this. I don't know how to let someone in like that. I've kept a part of myself hidden for so long, that I don't know how to be in a relationship. I've never been in a proper one because I was always afraid they would find out about me."

"Well, I know now so you don't have to hide it. And I'm sorry if anything I said made it harder for you. I was angry with myself and didn't want you to know that you were right, and I should never have gotten into the cage with that monster. I'm not good at this either, yano. So, maybe, just maybe, we say fuck it and learn how to do this together. What do you say?"

Shane wanted to cling to Eve's words, to envision a future for the two of them. He'd always put any thoughts of happiness on the back burner because he had this massive secret looming over him. Eve didn't pity him, he could tell the difference between her feeling sad that he'd been treated so badly by his dad, and pity. She was willing to fight for him, even after knowing all about him.

That meant Shane could do the same.

"I'd kiss you right now, but I know my breaths gotta be awful."

Eve grinned, lifting his hand to her lips. "You can kiss me later when everyone is gone. And if you feel too tired, you can just lay down and let me do all the work."

Shane laughed, stopping abruptly when a rap sounded on the bedroom door.

Andi opened the door, and took a step inside. Shane opened his mouth to say something, but she held up her hand. "I'm sorry, Carter. I reacted badly because I was worried. I care about you, you stubborn bastard. I want to understand. I want you to talk to me. But I know sometimes talking to family doesn't help and you need an outside perspective. I hope this is okay."

Andi took a step to the side and a curvy brunette that seemed vaguely familiar to Shane came in, a smile lighting up her face. "Hello, Shane. My name is Sinéad. You might know my fiancé, Jameson Kent?"

Shane nodded, slightly confused, and he looked from the woman to Andi. "What's going on?"

Andi put her hand on Sinéad's shoulder. "Sinéad is a trained counsellor. She's helped Jameson deal with his panic attacks. She's also been a sounding board for everyone that was held hostage in Rebel Books a couple of months ago. She's a very good listener."

The panic Shane had managed to quash earlier came back, and he wanted out of his own skin. It must have shown on his face because Sinéad held up her hands. "This is your choice, Shane. You have the control here. You make the decisions. If all you want to do is sit in silence and say nothing, I'm here for that. Nothing you say or do leaves this room."

Shane didn't know why he believed Sinéad, but he did. There was something about her voice that made him feel at ease. Eve squeezed his hand. "I can stay."

Shane had been afraid most of his life, and now, he wanted to do this for him. by himself.

"I got this but thank you."

Eve kissed his knuckles, and then she and Andi left him alone with Sinéad. They sat in relative silence for ages, until Shane felt like he just wanted to unburden himself.

"Things got worse after my mother left us..."

Chapter Twenty-Eight

Eve

SHANE AND SINEAD had been holed up in his bedroom for hours now, and when Eve had left them to come into the living room, the carnage that had been the evidence of Shane's relapse had been cleaned up. Eve had plonked down on the sofa, taking the offer of a tea when Sorcha offered it to her.

Ronan had been sitting on the chair, his head in his hands. Sorcha had looked worried about him, and it was obvious that Ronan had kept Shane's bulimia to himself. And while it must have been a terrible thing for Shane to carry, it must have been a massive burden for Ronan to carry too.

"He's lucky to have you, Ronan," Eve told him, and when he looked up from his hands, Eve could see that his eyes were red.

"I should have seen the signs. I should have known coming back here would trigger him. He's been good, really good for a while. The last time it was this bad was when everyone in Manchester found out he used to be a gymnast."

"That's why he went A.W.O.L for a while? He'd relapsed?" Andi had asked, and Ronan nodded.

"Ya. It was. What his dad did to him, it was awful. I fucking despise that man."

Eve was with Ronan on that one.

They had ordered some food, and Declan had come over to repair the door, asking Andi if she wanted him to stay and Andi had hugged him, telling him she'd call him. Andi had walked him out, telling them she needed to call Charlie and tell her. When she came back, carrying the food, her eyes were also red from crying.

They had dished up the food, and Ronan set some to the side in case they could get Shane to eat at some stage. Ronan explained that it would be slow for Shane, coming out of the relapse each time was different. That he might overcompensate for eating more with excessive working out. Eve listened intently to everything Ronan told her so that she could understand more of what Shane might need from her.

"Do you think I should send him back to Manchester?"

Ronan had shaken his head. "Sending him away now that you know might validate his feelings of low self-worth. He could interpret it as you wanting rid of him because you now know about his bulimia."

Andi had blinked. "Shit, I didn't even think about that. Fuck, okay."

They'd all felt a little uneasy about eating, especially when the door to the bedroom had opened and Sinéad came out. The woman might be smiling, but Eve could see it in her eyes whatever Shane had been telling her was having an effect on her.

"Shane could smell the food and we were wondering if there was any going spare."

Ronan had bolted upright, telling them he'd sort a plate

for him, that he knew what Shane liked. Sinéad had stopped him with a hand on his arm. "You've been the best friend he needed, Ronan. It would have been way worse had he not had you. He knows that. He said you kept him alive."

A sob had escaped Ronan then, and Sinéad had hugged him until Sorcha came over and took Sinéad's place. "Come on, Cusack. Let's get some air."

"I don't want to leave him. I wasn't here when he was struggling."

Sorcha snorted and patted his chest. "We're just stepping outside for a second. I'm sure the MMA fighter and Andi can give us the heads up if he needs you. Come on. Ten minutes. Please."

Ronan had nodded, still fixing a plate and handing it to Sinéad, who herself had declined any food. She walked back into the room and closed the door. Ronan and Sorcha had gone outside, leaving her and Andi alone. They didn't speak at all, just sat there. Andi was on her phone, a serious expression on her face.

When Ronan and Sorcha came back in, he sat down on the chair and closed his eyes. He was asleep a second later and Sorcha went about tidying up. Eve dozed herself, exhausted both physically and mentally. This wasn't how she expected her day to end, but she was glad that everything was out in the open now.

About an hour or so after Sinéad had taken the food to Shane, she emerged from the bedroom and closed the door softly behind her. The sound made Ronan jerk awake. Sinéad came in and took a seat, suppressing a yawn and taking the coffee Sorcha handed her.

"He's asleep. He fell asleep halfway through a sentence. His body just needs to rest and getting shit off your chest can be exhausting. I'm not gonna tell you guys everything, but from what he said, there is a lot of the abuse he didn't tell anyone. They never addressed his issues and it got worse. I'm happy to continue working with him. Shane had to make the decision himself to get better."

Sinéad went home a little while later, with plans to come back in a day or two when Shane had rested long enough to talk again. She had advised them to follow Shane's lead and not to push him to eat. He'd eaten half of what Ronan had put on his plate, which was a good start.

They'd all settled in for the night, but Eve told Andi to go home, and offered her apartment to Sorcha and Ronan. Ronan had refused to leave and Sorcha said she wanted to stay too so in the end they had all had a sleepover. Eve had lain on the floor, staring at the ceiling for hours, half afraid to go to sleep.

At about five in the morning, she gave up on sleep, and got up to make some coffee. She put on some toast, then hopped up on the breakfast bar. Her heart galloped when she heard Shane's bedroom door open and then the bathroom door closed. Eve was terrified he was gonna go in and purge again but after a minute or two the door opened and then Shane was standing just off the kitchen.

He was wearing shorts and a tee, his feet bare. His eyes looked tired, and he looked sort of anxious. He spotted Eve perched on the counter, quietly moving toward her. He hesitated for a second, but Eve placed her palms on the side of his neck. "Hey."

"Hey back."

Shane rolled his eyes. "You guys just had a slumber party. This is not how I envisioned all the hot women sleepovers in my head."

"Ha! Not enough pillows, Abercrombie?"

Shane chuckled, bracing his hands on either side of her on

the counter and then he lowered his mouth to hers. She could taste his toothpaste, felt the heat in his kiss like he was trying to gauge her reaction to him. The toast popped, and Shane pulled back sheepishly.

"Thank you," he said softly resting his head against hers.

Eve snorted, rolling her eyes. "Oh ya, it's a real hardship kissing you, Abercrombie. A real fucking hardship."

"Not for the kiss, ya idiot. For everything else."

"No need for thanks, Shane. We all just want you healthy and happy. And I want to see you naked again for purely selfish reasons but that's just me."

Shane barked out a laugh, then backed away, getting the toast, and then getting the butter from the fridge. Eve took it from him, then buttered it and took a bite. She remembered what Sinéad had said, but the way Shane was looking at the toast, Eve felt like she had to say something. It was like he needed permission to actually want to eat the food.

"You want the other slice?" Shane blinked, and Eve went on. "Or I can make some more if you want your own?"

She dangled her own toast in front of him and was surprised when he leaned down and took a bite of her slice. She didn't hesitate to throw the rest in her mouth as Shane went to make himself once of his shakes, then she felt hopeful as he took a nutrition bar out of the cupboard and ate it.

Baby steps. Shane was taking tiny baby steps and Eve would stand with him in case he needed help. They all would. His road to recovery would probably be long and hard, and yet, Eve was all in. She was all in this with him.

Because you love him...

Damn, she did, didn't she? She loved Shane. However, Eve knew that she would keep this to herself for now, wait for the right time, when he was ready. There was no rush to tell him. they had the rest of their lives for I love yous.

Shane came over to her then, having eaten his bar and

wrapped his arms around her. He didn't say anything, just held her, and she held him. There was no need for words the way he held her, none at all. Eve would deck anyone who dared hurt him again, but for now, she would just hold the man she loved tightly, never wanting to let him go.

CHAPTER TWENTY-NINE

Shane

TWO WEEKS HAD GONE by since everyone had found out about his eating disorder and the world hadn't imploded. Eve had stayed with him the last two weeks, and when she wasn't there or went to train, Ronan showed up to babysit him.

He'd gotten frustrated about three days in and told everyone to fuck off and leave him alone. Shane had felt like he needed to breathe, and everyone was making him feel like he was suffocating. Sinéad had told him it was because he had been internalizing everything and dealing with it on his own that having others to lean on felt weird, and strange, and he tended to go on the defensive.

It made complete sense to him, but he still needed time to himself.

This morning, he'd gotten out of bed, leaving Eve curled up sound asleep and walked the short distance down the road to Little Leaps. He hadn't bothered to check the time, and when he arrived, it was to see kids heading in the door and he stopped dead.

Mrs. Ryan spotted him and called him over. Shane went because she had been good to him, and she ushered him instead before he could protest. There were a lot of little eyes on him, and even the teachers were looking at him like they were starstruck.

Shane wanted to run away so bad.

"I missed you the last couple of weeks." Mrs. Ryan said as she stood next to him.

"I...I was unwell." That was the easiest way Shane could explain it without telling the other woman all about him.

"Oh, I'm sorry to hear that. Are you better now?"

"No. But I'm getting there."

And that was the God's honest truth.

Mrs. Ryan smiled at him and asked him if he wanted to do what he usually did, and she must have sensed his apprehension because she said. "This is a safe space, Shane. No one here is gonna judge you. Though you might get some admiring glances when they realize how good you are."

She left him standing there then to make up his mind and since he was feeling so restless, his mind racing, Shane decided to just say fuck it, and he started to stretch, his limbs feeling achy from the lack of exercise. For two weeks, he'd stayed away from exercise, working on eating right and getting his head right, but he had missed working out. It was an integral part of who he was and now that he was here, on the mats, Shane realized that he wanted to be here.

He started out small, doing a few rotations on the beam, because that was safe territory. He then moved to another apparatus, trying to ignore the crowd that had started to gather whenever he was on an apparatus.

The only thing he shied away from was the rings. Shane stood underneath them, images of his failure playing out in his mind, and he wanted to run to the nearest bathroom and get rid of the breakfast he'd eaten this morning.

Sinéad had sat with Shane the other day and told him that in order for him to heal in the way that he needed to, Shane needed to face the demons that held him back because he gave them so much power. The two things that terrified Shane were getting back on the rings and his dad.

Right here, right now, he could try and conquer one of those fears and get back on the rings for the first time since the Olympics. Shane chalked up his hands, trying to block out the onlookers as he closed his eyes, blew out a breath, and used one of the springboards to jump upwards.

The moment his fingers gripped the rings, Shane felt a mixture of relief and joy, laced with a hint of fear. The routines drilled into him from an early age played out in his mind and his body started to move. He did all the things he used to do, though not as strongly as he once did. The feeling of being invincible spread out in his chest when he got enough momentum to swing around, and there wasn't a sound in the gymnasium.

When he dismounted, landing with a foot out, not cleanly enough for his liking, and looked around, there was a lull of silence before people started clapping and cheering. Shane ducked his head in embarrassment and then he heard a shrill whistle, and he looked over to see Eve and Andi watching him.

Eve was grinning and Andi had her mouth open in shock.

Shane nodded his head at all the other gymnasts, walking over to Eve and Andi, who was staring at him.

"Damn, Carter, that was fucking epic."

"I didn't stick the landing and the handstand should have been held longer. But considering I haven't been on um since Rio, it's not bad."

Eve went up on her toes and kissed him. "You have no idea how sexy you look right now."

Shane laughed before folding his hands over his chest. "Did you guys follow me?"

Andi held up her hand not looking one bit guilty. "I followed you and then when I saw where you were going, I called Eve. I'm glad we did. That's some epic shit right there."

"Shane?"

Shane turned to see the woman who his dad had been with that day standing there, a warm smile on her face. "Hi. I'm sorry, I never got your name."

"Sharon. I wanted to thank you. For what you said that day. I asked my daughter, and she told me everything that had happened. Then your dad more or less admitted it himself. We left him, and I reported him to Gymnastics Ireland in case he had pulled that crap on other kids."

Shane swayed a little. Sharon reached for him, gave his arm a squeeze. "I know what he did to you, and I am so sorry for that. I think someone would like very much to meet her big brother."

Shane didn't know what to say. He was overwhelmed that his dad was now getting what he deserved, and he had spared another child going through what the trauma he did. He wasn't sure though that he was emotionally ready for being a big brother.

"That's my baby girl on the beam. She watched you do that spinny thing and now wants to try and do it herself. I told her all about you and she said she hoped that she got some of your genes so she could be just like you."

Fucking hell, the kid didn't need to be like him. He was a piss poor role model.

"I told her that it was you who told me what her dad might be doing, and she wanted to thank you. She saw you this morning but was scared to say hi. I know it's a lot, but she's only six and doesn't understand it all."

Well, how the fuck could he say no now without looking like a prick?

Shane looked at Eve and Andi, who both gave him a

thumbs up and Shane went with Sharon to where the girl was stood on the beam. She jumped down when they arrived, her eyes wide with excitement.

"Hi, I'm Ava." She said shyly and Shane could see that they looked sort of alike.

"I'm Shane." He crouched down to be at her level.

She laughed, a joyous sound and Shane knew that their father hadn't damaged her too much. She'd gotten out in time.

"I know that silly. You're my brother. All my classmates are very jealous. It's awesome."

Shane laughed then at her cheeky grin. "Is that so?"

"Yup, I told them that we were going to go for ice-cream some day and you were gonna help me make it to the Olympics if I trained really, really hard."

Shane's heart sank. Maybe he'd been wrong. Maybe Henry had some influence on the kid.

"But training hard doesn't mean I can't have cake and ice-cream and chicken nuggets. That's what mam said. Do you like chicken nuggets?"

Shane nodded, and then Ava threw herself at him, sending him to his ass as she hugged him. "I knew you would. We can have chicken nuggets and you can teach me all the amazing tricks. My brother will be better than everyone else's."

Shane didn't know what to say to all of that, so he just held her until she was called to her class and Shane exchanged numbers with her mam, knowing he wanted to be there for his sister in any way he could. Sharon hugged him then, thanking him again for what he had done, and Shane knew how to make peace with the things his dad did. He'd make sure Ava achieved anything she wanted in spite of Henry.

He strode over to Eve, who was grinning like she'd won the lotto, and Andi who punched him on the shoulder. "You softy."

He laughed, rolling his eyes. Eve slipped her hand into his

and gave it a squeeze as she said. You fancy going for something to eat? It's almost lunchtime."

They looked at him expectantly, so Shane tilted his head. "Is it weird to say I have a craving for chicken nuggets? I think I was Ava's age the last time I had um."

Eve gave him a smile that made his pulse race. "Anything you want, Abercrombie. Anything at all."

Chapter Thirty

Shane

One Month Later

Shane had never felt healthier in his life.

Or happier.

He'd decided to put himself first and do whatever he could to ensure that he didn't relapse. Shane had regular catch up's with Sinéad, had a frank and honest conversation with Andi and Charlie, assuring them that he'd tell them if he felt he was slipping. He'd gone for a pint or two with Ronan and Connor, the paramedic fitting into his and Ronan's dynamic like a pro and he told them it was because he was a triplet.

Shane had kept his promise and taken Ava and her mam for chicken nuggets. They were his newest obsession, something Eve had taken great amusement in, roaming shops to get the weirdest shaped nuggets she could. Like dinosaurs and shit.

He smiled at the memory, Eve's steady presence keeping him on the straight and narrow. They trained together too now that he had enlisted one of the personal trainers at the gym to help him with a rigorous but healthy training schedule.

Shane had also continued to go to Little Leaps for fun, and Mrs. Ryan kept getting him to help with the students, and she wouldn't take no for an answer. She'd asked him if he would like to come full time, and he had answered her honestly that he was having fun being here and if he did it full time, then it might not be fun anymore and he wasn't sure that was the right choice for him.

She'd understood completely, then offered him two afternoons a week, telling Shane to think it over before he made any decisions. She hadn't mentioned it again, and Shane was happy to push the offer to the back of his mind.

After the chicken nugget episodes, Eve had come into his apartment one afternoon armed with a notebook and a pen. She hoisted herself on the kitchen counter, given him a look that made him want to drag her off to bed, before she said. "Since we now have discovered your new obsession with nuggets, I think we should write a list of everything you ever wanted to eat and drink and go through the list."

"Eve," Shane had said, loving her for making the effort, but afraid it would set him back.

"Before you say no, I asked Sinéad and she said making the experience fun might make your brain associate eating in a new way."

Shane had watched as Eve opened the fridge, taken out the ice-cream she liked, and then yanked off her t-shirt. She stuck her fingers in and then put some on the curve of her breast, before licking her fingers.

He had to admit the sex they'd had there on the kitchen counter had been a lot of fun.

Shane was honest with the people around him when he was struggling now. When he and Eve had gone to dinner at Ronan and Sorcha's, he'd suddenly been hit with a wave of anxiety, and couldn't eat the food. Sorcha had just laughed and promised him that she hadn't cooked it, then went into the kitchen with him and asked him what he wanted.

He understood now why Ronan had fallen in love with her.

No one made him feel awkward during his recovery and Shane knew he should have been honest with people long ago. He wasn't ashamed anymore of his illness, and had even spoken to some of the young teenage boys at Little Leaps about having a healthy attitude toward food.

Andi and Charlie had been great too. They didn't bring anything up unless he did, and it was like nothing had ever happened. Andi asked him if he wanted to go back to Manchester, saying she would find a way that he could work from there if he wanted, but Shane told her he needed not to run away from his issues anymore.

Shane had wanted to work his ass off to get Eve the push she deserved. He'd called in every favour, every little bit of pull that he had in the sports industry and she would get her shot with a proper fight in six months in the UK, and if she did well, which she would, there might just be a UFC contract at the end of it.

Shane had been slowly building a portfolio of clients here in Ireland, and since he couldn't do it all, he'd interviewed one new staff member and was working his way through some more applications. The future for Rebel PR was gonna be damn bright and he was happy to be a part of it.

Today, Shane was in his office, having just finished up a call with Jack O'Neill, the rally driver Noah Donovan had signed and who Rebel PR were gonna represent when Andi and Charlie came into his office.

He should have known from their expressions they were up to something.

"Why do I feel like you two have been up to no good?" Shane said with a weary expression.

"Because you know us too damn well, Carter."

Charlie smacked Andi on the arm. "Behave. This is a serious work conversation."

Andi rolled her eyes and Charlie was grinning. They exchanged a look, and Shane shifted in his seat. "Am I being fired?"

Andi laughed. "Fuck no. You've made the company more money in the last month than we have in a while. I'm not stupid so we've decided to make sure no one can steal you away."

Shane looked at Charlie. "What the fuck is Collins on about?"

Resting her hands on her belly, Charlie sighed. "Right, since Andi's making an absolute mess of it, I'm gonna just spit it out." Charlie handed him a contract. "This is a new contract of employment. Both myself and Andi are giving you ten percent ownership of Rebel PR. We will retain forty percent each, but you will have shares in the company and become a stakeholder."

Shane glanced down at the contract. "Why would you do that? You guys made it happen."

"We made it happen with input from you. The dream was always to come home and run things here. Now you're home, you deserve to share in our success too. So, will you sign it and become a boss ass bitch with us?"

Shane barked out a laugh, taking the contract in his grasp. "This is too much. I can't accept this."

"Well, you signing is only a formality. I lodged all the other paperwork this morning so leaving you chose was a courtesy. Just sign the damn contract, Carter, 'cause we have something else to show you."

Shane rolled his eyes, wondering what the hell he was

getting himself into, but he signed the contract. Andi then informed him as an owner, he could pretty much set his own hours so he could take Mrs. Ryan up on her offer, if he wanted.

He had no clue how Andi found shit out...but she'd make one hell of a spy.

And then Andi was pulling him out of the office and into the reception area. Recently, the girls had put up pictures of everyone with famous people who were aligned with Rebel PR, and memorabilia they'd received. Shane roamed his eyes over the frames and came to a dead halt when he saw the newest additions to the wall.

He had no clue how Andi had found his medals, but there they were, in a fancy display frame on the wall, next to pictures of him at various competitions. Memories flashed through his mind as he heard Andi say softly.

"We wanted you to know that we are proud of your achievements. And you should be too. If it makes you feel uncomfortable, we can take them down but this is not something that should be hidden away."

Shane hadn't known what to say, he just asked where they had gotten them.

"Would you believe that Eve tracked your dad down and with Ronan and a very mouthy Sorcha in tow, they rocked up to your dad's place and demanded he hand over all your medals. I'd have paid to see it."

Shane had been standing there looking at the medals for ages after, and it was only when he felt arms go around his waist from behind that he dragged his gaze away. He turned to face her, and she grinned up at him. "Is that okay? I hope it's okay."

It was more than okay. It was the greatest gift anyone had given him.

Shane leaned down and kissed Eve hard on the mouth. "I love you."

Eve blinked, then she gave him a slow, sexy smile that heated the blood in his veins. "I love you too, Abercrombie. Now take me home so we can get naked."

Shane laughed, a lightness in him as he realized she loved him back, and no medal or podium could ever match the feeling of being loved by Eve. He didn't need a gold medal, Shane realized, putting that ghost to bed, because he'd struck gold by falling in love with Eve.

He had already won.

THE END

The Rebel County Universe Stories continue in
Drive Me Crazy (Rebel PR Book 2)

Find More Rebel Stories On Kindle Vella

Take The Lead is the third book in the Rebel Books Trilogy. Rebel Books is part of the Rebel County Universe which will span at least four different businesses, with intersecting time-lines, and characters popping up when you least expect them.

The Rebel Racers Trilogy
Available Now:
Adrenaline Junkie (Rebel Racers Book 1)
All or Nothing (Rebel Racers Book 2)
Crash and Burn (Rebel Racers Book 3)

The Rebel Rock Trilogy
Available Now:
Centre Stage (Rebel Rock Book 1)
Strings Attached (Rebel Rock Book 2)
Make or Break (Rebel Rock Book 3)

The Rebel Ink Trilogy
Available Now:
Breaking the Habit (Rebel Ink Book 1)
Uncomfortably Numb (Rebel Ink Book 2)
Secrets In Ink (Rebel Ink Book 3)

The Rebel Books Trilogy
Available Now:
Best Laid Plans (Rebel Books Book 1)
More Than Words (Rebel Books Book 2)
Take The Lead (Rebel Books Book 3)

The Rebel PR Trilogy
Available Now:
Sucker For Pain (Rebel PR Book 1)
Drive Me Crazy (Rebel PR Book 2)

Playlists

Shane

Twenty One Pilots - Jumpsuit

Lil Wayne - Sucker for Pain (with Wiz Khalifa, Imagine Dragons, Logic & Ty Dolla $ign feat. X Ambassadors)

Liily - Applause

Puddle Of Mudd - She Hates Me

James Arthur - Maybe

Plested - Beautiful & Brutal

Dead Poet Society - How could I love you?

Dead Poet Society - I hope you hate me.

Adele - Hometown Glory

Dermot Kennedy - Homeward

Sleep Token - Blood Sport

The Struts - Could Have Been Me

Jeremy Renner - Main Attraction

Loveless - happier than ever

The Unlikely Candidates - Novocaine

Bryce Fox - Golden Boy

grandson - Riptide

Saint Chaos - Ghosts & Monsters

Eminem - Guts Over Fear Ft Sia

YUNGBLUD - Happier (feat. Oli Sykes of Bring Me The Horizon

The Score - Stronger

James Vincent McMorrow - I Lie Awake Every Night

Alessia Cara - Scars To Your Beautiful

Mother Mother - I Go Hungry

Garbage - Bleed Like Me

Skylar Grey - Invisible

Billie Eilish - listen before i go

Nico Santos - Play With Fire

Des Rocs - Used to the Darkness

grandson - Dirty

TLC - Unpretty

Eve

Eve - Who's That Girl?
Tommee Profitt - I'll Carry You
Andreya Triana - Heart In My Hands
The Score - Fighter
Eminem - Till I Collapse
YONAKA - Punch Bag
YONAKA - Teach Me To Fight
Billie Eilish - Lost Cause
Billie Eilish - Happier Than Ever
SATV Music - We Be Going Hard
flowerovlove - a girl like me
Fall Out Boy - I Don't Care
Bohnes - Middle Finger
The Unlikely Candidates - Oh My Dear Lord
Barns Courtney – Champion
Måneskin - GASOLINE
Måneskin - DON'T WANNA SLEEP
Blame My Youth - Fantastic
Nothing But Thieves - Honey Whiskey
Sam Tinnesz - Bloodshot
R U Init - Original Sound
Everyone You Know - All My Friends Are Taking Drugs
The Struts - Too Good At Raising Hell
Fort Minor - Remember the Name (feat. Styles of Beyond)
Kendrick Lamar - HUMBLE.
M.I.A. - Bad Girls
Halsey - Gasoline
Architects - Seeing Red
Lady Gaga - Applause
Lovejoy - Normal People Things
Dermot Kennedy - The Corner

Acknowledgments

None of this would be possible without an amazing team supporting me! Many thanks to:

Publishing House: CTP Publishing
Cover design: Gem Promotions
Interior Formating: Gem Promotions

———

And as always:
Thank you to all the readers!
Whether this is your first book by me or you've been with me for years! I only get to do this because of you, and I am eternally grateful to each and every one of you who took a chance on this Irish author.

ABOUT THE AUTHOR

Susan Harris is a writer from Cork, Ireland and when she's not torturing her readers with heart-wrenching plot twists or killer cliffhangers, she's probably getting some new book related ink, binging her latest TV or music obsession, or with her nose in a book.

Susan LOVES connecting with her fans!
www.susanharrisauthor.com

Also by Susan Harris

The Wings Of Deceit Series

Angel's Gambit, book 1

Angel's Rebel, book 2

Angel's Traitor, book 3

The Ever Chace Chronicles

Skin & Bones, book 1

Collateral Damage, book 2

Smoke & Mirrors, book 3

Night of the Hunter, book 4

Never Back Down, book 5

Shortcut to the Grave, book 6

Arsonist's Lullaby, book 7

Of Gods & Monsters, book 8

———

Shattered Memories

———

Defy The Stars

A Tale of Two Houses, book 1

Until Death Do Us Part, book 2

In Defiance of the Stars, book 3

Courting Darkness, a novella

The Sanguine Crown

Chaos Theory, book 1

Butterfly Effect, book 2

Wicked Game, book 3

Burn Notice, book 4

Fight Song, book 5

The Sicarius Security Series

Kiss Of Death, book 1

Leap Of Faith, book 2

Visions Of Destiny, book 3

War Of Hearts, book 4

Flames Of Conflict, book 5

Anthology

A Lot Like Christmas

The Murdering Hour Novels

Own The Night, book 1

Dwell In Darkness, book 2